RVing America
Through the Eyes of
Honeybee The Cat

Fulltiming

by
Honeybee

Since 1974

PO Box 221974 Anchorage, Alaska 99522-1974

ISBN 1-59433-018-2

Library of Congress Catalog Card Number: 2004114644

Manufactured in the United States of America.

2

Dedication

Honeybee dedicates Fulltiming to Reverend and Mrs. James Turner Higgins.

Acknowledgment

A special thanks to Ann, Judy, and Charlene.

3

Table of Contents

Chapter I
My Darkest Moment

I couldn't believe my parents were really and truly leaving me behind. I watched as my father, looking straight ahead, eyes moist and reddened, trying to be strong for my mother's sake, started our big two-tone brown truck and pulled back onto the Alcan. Our little blue and white trailer, one of the five in which I had spent the last twelve years of my life and traveled half a million miles, followed along behind, bouncing through the chuckholes in the pullout beside Teslin Lake. I could see my mother crying. I knew her heart was breaking, as was mine. She couldn't see me, but I could see her. I could see her looking back and still crying when they disappeared over the horizon. Only now did I realize I would never see my parents again. I sat and continued to stare down the highway long after they had gone, hoping to see them one more time, just one last glimpse. As the vastness and stillness of the Yukon settled over me, so did reality.

They were not my real parents, but I couldn't have loved

them more. My biological mother, although a bit flirtatious, was very sophisticated, with impeccable breeding. There are some questions, however, about my father. It has been rumored he was a handsome and daring young bandito who stole across the San Ysidro-Tijuana border and trekked the sands of Coronado's Silver Strand in the dark of the moon just to be with my mother. And there were the stories about her late-night rendezvous with a certain city slicker who stowed away on the ferries crossing Glorietta Bay from San Diego. Then there were the midnight strolls on the beach with a mysterious young sailor from North Island Naval Air Station. I have only blurred and distant memories of my biological mother and my references to her love affairs are strictly hearsay. I will probably never learn the true identity of my father or why I was put up for adoption, nor do I care. These things are important only because they account for my birth and for the turn of fate that brought me and my parents, the only parents I've ever known, together.

My mother fell in love with me at first sight and I with her. Back then, my parents owned a small house in Bonita, California with a big yard and lots of trees; this is where I grew up. Although Bonita was only about twenty miles from the place where I was born in Coronado, it had a country flavor with horses, cows, chickens, and a stream-fed lake with lots of ducks, and, unlike the city, very little traffic. One could cross the street without concerning oneself with speeding motorists; on our street hours passed with greater regularity than cars.

The backyard was divided by rock walls and shrubbery into what I considered the upper and lower yard. Most of the trees grew in the backyard. I climbed them all, over and over again. Actually, climbing a tree was how I got my name.

It was early afternoon on my first day with my new parents and I was just learning to climb. From the very beginning I had absolutely no fear of climbing and had ventured way out on the limb of a tree with lots of nice-smelling little white flowers. Bees hummed everywhere, buzzing from one blossom to another. Having never seen a bee, I was curious and ventured quite close while trying to touch one with my paw. When I finally succeeded, the bee made it very clear he was busy and didn't have time to play and suggested, in no un-

6

certain terms, I should go climb another tree. My parents were nearby on the patio, eating lunch, and when I cried out from pain and went into full reverse, trying to avoid another sting, my father laughed and said, "Well, I guess you learned not to mess around with the honeybees." That's when my mother decided to name me Honeybee.

In the days of my youth my backyard seemed very large and it appeared to me at least half the trees in the world grew there. But after a half million miles of crisscrossing North

Even in southern California a fire during the winter months sometimes felt good. I sat by the fire every chance I got—perhaps that is why I love campfires so much.

America traveling up and down, back and forth, from San Diego to Moosonee, Key West to Prudhoe Bay, I learned the backyard of my childhood was very small. At almost every stop along those half million miles I climbed a tree. I climbed more trees than I can ever count.

I remember one in particular early on in my travels, a tall pine in upstate New York on Lake Champlain. When chased by a big dog I climbed clear to the top and refused to come down. Actually I was scared. I had never been chased before. My mother, suspecting my anxiety, slept underneath the tree that night until I decided to come down.

7

But I'm getting ahead of myself. It all began, my travels that is, almost six months earlier, just a few days after my third birthday. When awakening from one of my naps, I spotted a small silver house beside the garage. It was certainly funny looking with dark windows on all sides and only one door. But, strangest of all, it had wheels. I couldn't imagine what it was for or who would want to live in such a silly-looking house. My mother was busy, making trip after trip, carrying clothes, food, dishes, and things I didn't even know we owned from our house to the little silver house. I was curious, as is my nature, and after inspecting its exterior I climbed slowly and cautiously up the two steps hanging down from beneath the door, and stuck my head inside. It smelled peculiar; nevertheless, I decided to explore its interior. It appeared very unstable, rocking back and forth with my every step. It did, however, have advantages; by walking along the backs of the two couches, the kitchen counters, and the bathroom vanity, I could easily see everything outside and in all directions. I later learned the glass was designed to let me see out while preventing anyone outside from seeing me. After inspecting everything I decided it was time for another nap and climbed onto the back of a couch and fell asleep under the warm rays of the afternoon sun.

It must have been about two weeks later when early one Saturday morning I was awakened by an unfamiliar noise. From my chair by the dining room window where I had been dozing I noticed a crowd of people gathering in the front yard. My parents didn't seem all that concerned, although they were anxiously watching the clock while finishing their morning coffee. At exactly eight o'clock my father opened the door to the breezeway connecting the house to the garage. And almost before he could move aside, people started streaming into the house, pushing past one another grabbing at our things and yelling, "How much?" Afraid of getting squashed, I headed for the garage and, I presumed, safety. I had presumed too much. I hurried through the side door and realizing something was amiss, instinctively scampered underneath a workbench. My father had just opened the big car door and people were everywhere, grabbing stuff and asking the same question, "How much?" Then I noticed they were

8

carrying our things outside and putting them into their cars and driving away. The first time I thought I could safely make it to the door I dashed outside and found people carrying away everything in the yard. They were hauling off potted plants and chairs from the patio. Two guys were carrying away our picnic table. And, to make things worse, every time one vehicle would leave another would pull up and a new group would come rushing into the house or garage. Well, I'd had enough of this nonsense; I headed for the upper back-yard and a tree.

After about an hour I spotted my friend Butch walking along the wall separating his yard from ours. I climbed down as quickly as I could and joined him on the wall. I never knew his real name; everyone always called him Butch, probably because of his appearance. He had lived a hard life and it showed. Butch just appeared one day from out of nowhere and after a few weeks of roaming the neighborhood moved in with the nice family next door. At first he kept pretty much to himself, but over time, we had become good friends. Except for the stories he told about all the people he had known, the places he had been, and the things he had seen, no one knew anything about his past, but everyone liked Butch and he was considered very wise. I told him about the strange goings on at my house and asked his opinion. He looked very serious and worried; after listening for a while, I under-stood why. Butch related a sad story about a similar situation that had taken place about a year earlier: Two men had shown up early one morning at his place and commenced loading his folks' things into a big truck and at the end of the day when everything was loaded they got into the truck and drove away. After the two men left with the truck carrying all his family's possessions his folks looked around the house, locked the doors, got into their car and they, too, drove away. They never came back. Butch had waited around for almost two months before giving up all hope of their return. Finally, he started searching for a new home. After several months and many hardships he found our neighborhood and moved in with the people next door.

As I lay stretched out on a limb, watching people carry our things away, I thought about all the things Butch had said

9

and was saddened when I recalled how emotional he became when relating the story about his folks moving away without him; he must have loved them very much. Although there were similarities in the goings-on at my house and the events that had taken place at Butch's house prior to the morning he found himself abandoned I wasn't worried; my parents would never leave me behind. By late afternoon things had settled down and I decided it was safe for me to go back into the house. I couldn't believe my eyes. The house was almost empty. My favorite chair was gone, along with the sofas, the beds, the dining room furniture, and the television; not one piece of furniture remained. All but a few of my parents' clothes were missing from the closet.

I sat on the hearth, dumbfounded, and watched my parents move the few remaining items into the garage. I thought about what Butch had told me and how his parents had left him behind and although I knew my parents would never abandon me, I suddenly became aware of a sick feeling in the pit of my stomach. I discounted it as nothing more than hunger pangs, but I knew it wasn't; it was something unfamiliar and unnerving. However, several hours had passed since I last ate, and out of habit I headed for my food dish. I panicked. My food and water dishes were both gone. Everything Butch told me flooded my mind. I was unable to think. Nausea almost overwhelmed me and my vision began to fade. Everything was turning black. I guess I was running around in circles crying when my mother stopped on the way back in from the garage, picked me up and held me in her arms. She asked where I had been, kissed me on the forehead and told me she had missed me. I knew right then everything was going to be alright. She took me inside the funny-looking little silver house and gently lowered me into the bathtub. To my surprise and delight, there was my food dish full of my favorite food, and right next to it was my water dish filled to the brim. She rubbed my head a couple of times before leaving; I knew she was busy so I just started eating as if nothing mattered.

I had finished eating and was preparing to leap out of the tub when I spotted a strange-looking box at the opposite end. The box was made of plastic and was about a foot and a half wide, two feet long, and six inches tall. The bottom of

10

the ugly yellow box had a two-inch layer of funny-looking, weird-smelling little rocks. I hadn't seen anything like it before and I pondered its purpose. Later, after eating my fill and consuming a large amount of water, I found myself locked inside the funny little house. How the box was to be utilized and by whom became obvious.

It had been a long and trying day and I was in need of a nap. I found the back of the couch in the warm afternoon sun perfect. I could doze and still keep an eye on the front yard. Detecting a slight movement of the little house, I opened one eye ever so slightly and saw Butch sitting just outside the window on what I later learned was the cover for two propane bottles. I also learned the little house was known as a recreational vehicle and referred to as a trailer. As it turned out, propane was the lifeblood of the little trailer; it was necessary for cooking, keeping the refrigerator cold, providing hot water, and furnishing heat when the weather turned chilly. There was even a propane lamp. I'm getting ahead of myself again.

I was glad to see my old friend; I needed someone to talk with and who better than Butch, the neighborhood sage. Although I knew my parents would never move away and leave me behind, as Butch's parents had done, the sad story he had related earlier with details of everything leading up to the morning he awoke and found himself abandoned, weighed heavily on my mind and I was not without anxiety.

My mother had left the window slightly open, for ventilation, so Butch and I were able to carry on a quiet conversation without attracting attention. Butch told of another friend, in his old neighborhood, whose parents had a similar little house built onto a truck. He remembered that every so often they would load lots of stuff into the little house and disappear for the weekend and leave his friend to fend for himself. Sometimes they would stay away for two weeks or even a month while his friend moped about the neighborhood begging food and getting on everyone's nerves. This latest story did little to reassure me; I could not imagine being separated from my parents for a whole month or even a week, still, it was better than forever.

That night we all slept in the little house; my father referred to it as the "Airstream." My parents were obviously exhausted

11

and slept very well. I, on the other hand, had too many things racing through my subconsciousness and slept very little, waking often. I tried to convince myself nothing bad was going to happen to me, but too many events of today paralleled the circumstances in Butch's life prior to the morning he found himself all alone; I was getting scared.

The next morning my worst fears were realized when a couple of men showed up and loaded the rest of our belongings into a truck, gave my father some money, and drove away. A short time later two more men arrived, my father handed over the keys to our house to one of the two men while the second guy erected a big sign on our front lawn. Curiosity demanded I walk over and take a look. The two largest words on the sign jumped out at me—it read, "For Sale." I panicked; my parents were selling our house. It was all true; everything I feared might happen was, indeed, happening. I was going to be left all alone, just like Butch, unloved and unwanted. I didn't know what to do; I just sat down and began to cry.

A few minutes passed before I noticed my father was hooking the trailer onto the back of our El Camino; they were almost ready to leave. The last few events had taken place in such rapid succession I'd had little time to think, but I had now recovered some of my wits and was determined not to be left behind. I would hide inside the Airstream and hope, once discovered, I would be able to convince them to change their minds. My mother, busy inside the trailer, didn't notice when I dashed through the open door and scooted behind the couch.

When my father finished hooking up the Airstream to the El Camino he walked around outside checking everything in detail before asking my mother, "You about ready?"

She replied that she was and then asked, "Where's Honeybee?"

"I saw her run inside just a couple of minutes ago."

"I don't see her," my mother stated as she began searching for me.

"I'm sure I saw her come inside," my father replied, as he looked behind the front couch—the couch to the right of the door, as you entered, positioned across the forward part of the Airstream, became known as the front couch.

12

"Well, you had better find her. We aren't going anywhere until you find her."

"Okay, I'll find her."

I panicked again. They were going to drag me out of my hiding place, throw me out into the yard, drive away and leave me. What was I going to do? I started to cry again.

My father was now peering behind the other couch, and directly at me.

"Here she is," he announced.

"Where?" my mother asked.

"There," my father pointed a finger in my direction. I snuggled into my hidey-hole as tightly as I could, trying to make myself invisible. But when my mother shone a flashlight behind the couch I knew it was all over and there was nothing more I could do. When she reached for me my heart stopped. I closed my eyes and waited.

Somehow, even then, in my darkest moment, I wasn't surprised when she patted me on the head and asked, "Are you okay?" It was then I knew all my fears were unfounded. I would never be left behind. I had no idea of what might happen next or where my parents were going, but, wherever it might be, I knew that I, too, would be going.

My parents left me where I had been hiding behind the couch, went outside and locked the Airstream door. A few minutes later I heard the El Camino's doors slam shut, I heard the engine start, and felt the sensation of movement. We were off. I couldn't explain the feeling that swept over me. Considering my emotional roller-coaster ride of the last couple of days, it seemed strange I would find leaving home exciting. Only the unknown lay before me. I should have been scared. So, why was I excited?

13

14

Chapter II
Runaway

The Airstream was in constant motion; it was either pitching and rolling, swaying back and forth, or bouncing up and down. The noise was annoying and sometimes frightening; dishes rattled in the cupboards, the tires screamed their rejection to contact with the pavement and the entire trailer creaked and groaned with every movement. And then there was inertia; I learned about inertia the hard way. The first time my father braked hard it threw me to the opposite end of the couch; then, as he accelerated again I was thrown back toward the other end. Now I knew why the manufacturer called their contraption a Land Yacht—it rode like a rowboat in a hurricane. I had pretty much lost track of time, I only knew I was hungry and thirsty, but I was afraid to try and reach my food dish for fear of being bounced off the wall and ending up with a concussion, a broken limb or worse. To further complicate things I was getting motion sickness.

Just about the time I thought I was going to throw up we began

15

slowing down and I started feeling better almost immediately. By the time we stopped I was feeling pretty good—all I needed was some fresh air, the kind you find high up in a tree. I formulated my plan. When the door opened I would dash outside and run up the tallest tree I could find. Considering the way I felt right now I just might stay up that tree forever. I'd already had enough of the Airstream to last me for the rest of my life, all nine of them.

I heard my father's footsteps as he approached, heard the key slip into the lock, and heard the bolt retract. I was already sitting by the door and at the moment it opened I was outside like a shot. As I streaked past my father I heard my mother yell, "Don't let Honeybee out!"

Fifty feet from the door I slid to a stop. I could see for miles in all directions and there wasn't a tree in sight. We were in the middle of a desert. About that time I heard my mother yell again, "Don't let her get away. Put her back inside."

Well I'd had enough of this nonsense. I wasn't going to be a prisoner for the rest of my life in some torture chamber on wheels. They could color me gone.

My father was almost on top of me before I had a chance to collect my thoughts. Acting on instinct, I bolted toward the only cover in sight, a patch of cactus along the edge of an arroyo about seventy-five yards away. At that time, of course, I had never heard of a desert, a cactus, or an arroyo. But I have learned much in my twelve years of living on the road. And, like Butch, I learned many lessons in the school of hard knocks. I imagine I could tell Butch some stories that would make him sit up and take notice, and probably one or two he wouldn't even believe.

My father chased after me, but in that short distance he stood no chance of catching me. My schooling at Hard Knocks High began in earnest when I sprinted past some century plants and scooted down into the arroyo. The long skinny leaves of the century plants were sharp as needles. The first one speared me in my right shoulder, a second one stabbed my other shoulder and a third one went deep into my left hip. I hit the bottom of the arroyo in an avalanche of rocks and sand, with my nose stuck in a prickly pear. The larger thorns of the prickly pear slashed open my nose and I had a mouthful of soft stickers that itched and burned.

16

I had just managed to untangle myself from the avalanche and prickly pear when I heard my father call down to me. I couldn't see him but I could hear him pacing back and forth at the edge of the arroyo. To make sure he wouldn't spot me, I crawled underneath one of the prickly pears, encountering more thorns in the process.

I was sick, tired, and hungry. My shoulders and hip were on fire and the more I rubbed my nose and mouth the more the stickers spread. I was miserable. I wanted to go home. I wanted to see my friend Butch. I wanted all this to be a bad dream. I wanted to wake up and find everything the way it used to be.

Both my parents were now walking back and forth along the arroyo's edge trying to coax me out; I didn't move or answer their calls. My father said, "Don't worry, she'll come out when she gets hungry." Finally, after what seemed like an eternity they went back to the trailer. I found a soft expanse of sand, warmed by the afternoon sun, and on this late spring day, tired, lonely, homesick, and in pain, I stretched out for a nap.

When I awoke, a giant moon hung in the sky so close I felt if I leaped really high I could touch it. The sky seemed larger than ever before and was full of twinkling stars. I had never seen so many. Birds sang as they flitted through the small trees, bushes, and cacti. Aromas of night-blooming flowers drifted about on a gentle breeze. What had earlier seemed like a place totally devoid of life was now alive with sounds and smells. I sat totally mesmerized for an incalculable time.

As the spell subsided it came to me by way of sharp, relentless hunger pangs. I had gone all day without food or water. But with this smorgasbord of critters running around it shouldn't be too difficult to rustle up a few tasty morsels.

Excited at the thought of a fat field mouse out there just waiting for me I began my customary stretch. I winced and cut my stretching short as pain shot through both my shoulders and my left hip. Also, my mouth was badly swollen. But the need for food prevailed and masked the pain as I set off on my quest.

A beetle passed within easy reach. Instinctively, I placed a paw on top of the hard-shelled little guy. He squirmed around

17

for a second or two before giving up, or so I thought. To my surprise, when I lifted my paw to take a peek, he had disappeared. I pounced on one of his relatives and found the scenario repeating itself. After a couple more attempts I found the vanishing act to be no mystery at all—the little critters had merely burrowed into the soft sand. They could swim through sand almost as easily as I could walk through air. Well, they didn't look all that tasty anyway.

As I sat, contemplating my next move, I spotted a skinny four-legged creature about six inches long, including his tail which was almost as long as his body. He lacked the mouth-watering appeal of a plump field mouse, but he would tide me over until something more appetizing presented itself. Carefully and silently I moved within range. I pounced with deadly accuracy. He moved with amazing speed and I was left with only his tail, still wiggling, between my paws while the rest of him scurried away to safety. I was too dumbfounded to give chase. Living here obviously required a different set of rules for survival than I was accustomed to; everyone seemed to have their own special technique. Apparently, it was going to be more difficult for me to survive in this environment than I had first imagined. Perhaps I had been a bit too hasty in my decision to run away.

Continuing, I encountered a giant hairy spider five or six inches in diameter. I gave him plenty of room. This guy looked dangerous and was about as appetizing as a Brillo pad. I had the distinct feeling that had he been twice his size he would have attacked me. I kept a sharp eye out for any of his friends that might be around and moved on down the arroyo.

A slight peripheral movement caught my attention, and suddenly things were looking up. A mouselike creature was busy collecting and eating seed from a few stalks of grass underneath a large saguaro. He was twice as big as any mouse I had ever seen and rather strange looking with large ears, long legs, and an extra long tail, tufted at the end. Regardless of his appearance, I suspected he would taste pretty much like all the other mice I had eaten. Here was a meal fit for a king. So as not to alert him to his destiny I crouched and stole forward without a sound. Unaware of my presence, he continued to munch on the grass seed. He was only six feet

18

away; he was mine. All set to pounce, I was waiting for the right moment, when, without warning, a blur streaking from out of nowhere and disappearing just as quickly struck a deadly blow. The mouse cried out just once and twitched only two or three times; seconds later he was dead. The large Red Diamondback Rattler slithered from the shadows to claim his victim. My heart raced as I realized mere seconds had separated me from the rodent's fate—I could have been the rattlesnake's dinner.

Moving silently so as not to attract the rattler's attention, I started back in the direction from which I'd come and began rethinking my earlier decision. There was plenty of good food and fresh water awaiting me in the trailer. My parents, who loved me, protected me, and provided for me waited there also. Perhaps I had been a bit hasty in running away. Already I had injured myself several times and only narrowly escaped death. My hunting skills had failed me and I had yet to find badly needed water. I was beginning to doubt I could survive without my parents. As I weighed love and security against life on my own, trailer life was beginning to look better with each passing second.

I was nearing the place where I had descended into the arroyo when I spotted another weird creature. When I approached he stopped and began moving back and forth in quick short steps. His long skinny tail was curled forward and held high above his head as he danced about. In order to examine the critter more closely I just naturally placed my paw on top of him. He slammed the tip of his tail down into the back of my paw and delivered the pain of a thousand bee stings. I became very weak and dizzy. My vision blurred and I was having trouble breathing. Well, enough was enough. The trials and tribulations of trailer living could not possibly compare to the pain and agony I had experienced these last few hours.

My decision made, I started climbing out of the arroyo when an alarming thought entered my mind. What if my parents had left without me? In a panic I headed for the top of the arroyo as fast as I could climb. I was oblivious to everything except the frightening imagery flashing across my consciousness. I could see myself going mad and dying all alone in this

19

hostile place. Focused on a single thought, to reach the Airstream before my parents left without me, I became careless and fell into the mouth of a large burrow. Startled, the burrow's owner bolted from his home knocking me all the way to the bottom of the arroyo. My heart stopped. I recovered slowly as I watched a large jackrabbit bounce along the arroyo's floor and disappear around a bend. After a couple of minutes my pulse slowed and my thoughts returned to the terrifying possibility that my parents had left without me and I was all alone in this wilderness, I would surely die. I wasted no time, although climbing more cautiously this time, in reaching the top of the arroyo. I sighed a sigh of relief as my fears were all swept away.

The Airstream stood less than a hundred yards away and I was almost certain the door was open. Well, this was not the time to speculate, I wanted to get across that expanse of open desert before anything else happened. I had taken only a couple of steps when I stopped, frozen in my tracks unable to move. I was terrified; my blood turned to ice. The coyote howled a second time, snapping me out of my trance. I spotted him off to my right silhouetted against the moon atop a rock outcropping about two hundred fifty to three hundred yards away. He howled again and this time, echoing out of the night came his mate's reply. I was no longer the hunter, I had become the hunted. I threw caution to the wind and streaked with wild abandon across what now looked like a distance of several miles, toward the open door of the Airstream. The desert floor was strewn with rocks and I had to dodge an occasional cactus. I knew I should keep my eyes in front of me at all times, otherwise I might trip and fall. A fall would cost me valuable seconds and might mean the difference between living and dying. Still, I chanced a glance toward the rock outcropping. The coyote was gone. I looked again. He was nowhere in sight. I knew he had spotted me as soon as I started across the open area and was, now, somewhere in the night, sprinting along a track meant to intersect mine before I could reach the Airstream. The pads of my feet were being torn to shreds on the sharp pieces of lava littering the desert floor. I was oblivious to all pain and tried to increase my speed beyond the impossible. My heart was pound-

20

ing so hard I was afraid it would explode. The Airstream was getting closer and closer, I was going to make it. The open door was only fifty feet away. If I slowed down at this realization it was only in my mind, and if I spurted ahead with twice the speed I was already going when I realized I was racing with a shadow, that, too, was only in my mind. The shadow swept along the ground, overtook me and moved slightly ahead. From five feet away I made a desperate leap with what I was sure was my last ounce of energy. To my surprise, I stopped in midair and was thrown backwards, bounced off the steps, and landed hard on my left side. The outside door was open, but in the dark the black screen mesh was invisible. Remembering the racing shadow, I scrambled underneath the trailer. Looking up I spotted a huge owl gliding along on silent wings, hunting from the sky for his dinner. I heard footsteps inside the Airstream. The screen door opened, and a mere heartbeat later I was in my hidey-hole.

22

Chapter III
On The Road

I don't know how long I slept, but when I awoke it was still dark. I didn't feel like moving, but I couldn't ignore the hunger pangs. The bottoms of my feet burned with each step I took. Both shoulders were stiff, my face was swollen so badly I could barely open my eyes and my right paw was as big as a baseball. Even my fur hurt. When I finally managed to get into the bathtub, eating, even lapping water became a new experience in pain.

I always made a lot of noise crunching my Purina Stars, and this morning was no different, but in the pre-dawn desert stillness the sound of my crunching seemed extra loud. It may have been these sounds that woke my mother or it may have been she was rising, as usual, for her morning run. She normally rose early and after a cup of coffee started her run just as dawn was breaking. Whatever the reason, she came in to see me. My mother loves the darkness almost as much as I do and never turns on a light in the morning, preferring to use a Mini-Maglite instead. As she knelt down by the tub I

23

stopped eating and looked up at her just as she shone the Maglite in my face. She took one look at me and gasped, then asked, "What happened to you?"

She promptly woke my father insisting he find a doctor right away. He convinced her that finding a veterinarian in Death Valley in the middle of the night would be next to impossible, but we could easily locate a veterinary clinic in Las Vegas, some two hundred miles away. Unless it had something to do with fishing, anytime before 8 a.m. was the middle of the night to my father. After some discussion they agreed to leave right after breakfast.

I didn't like going to the vet; they always poked, probed and stuck me with needles. But at the moment I'd willingly submit to anything that would make me feel better.

The clinic smelled like all the others I'd seen and patients waiting their turns were as unfriendly as usual, often snipping at one another for no reason. Eventually it became my turn and in addition to the poking, probing, and needle sticking the doctor tweezed stickers from my face, trickled some yucky stuff into my mouth, spread goo on all my cuts and taped tight-fitting socks on my feet. My mother continued to trickle the yucky stuff into my mouth every few hours and spread more goo on the pads of my feet twice a day.

We stayed in a campground behind the Circus Circus where at least two hundred other rigs were parked side by side all lined up in neat rows; I was reminded of a used-car lot. Apparently, no one stayed long. Several pulled out every day to be replaced by new arrivals. Why did these people choose to live in trailers and motor homes rather than real houses? Why were they always moving? Where were they going? What possessed my mother and father to leave home? I wanted to go back, but I wouldn't go back without them, even if I could. I loved them too much and even though it embarrassed me to admit it, I was dependent upon them. Las Vegas was nothing to get excited about, unless you liked bright lights and enjoyed watching people. Nobody ever seemed to sleep; they came and went at all hours, day and night. They passed my window one or two at a time, and in threes and fours, and sometimes in noisy groups. Many laughed as they passed, others appeared lost in deep thought while some looked grim

24

and dejected. I soon became bored with it all and spent most of the time sleeping. Almost a week passed before we visited the vet again. I guess there must be a law requiring veterinarians to stick you with at least one needle per visit. After the needle-sticking part, the doctor gave my mother some more gooey stuff and another bottle of the yucky-tasting liquid and we were on our way. On our way to where? I didn't know. I was hoping we were going home, but that was not to be.

At our next stop, the Valley of Fire, I had a most humiliating experience. My mother strapped me into a very uncomfortable

It all started, my mother's attempt to have me follow her on a leash, when I ran away at the first rest stop on our first day of RV-ing. The fact that I reconsidered my decision and returned to the Airstream later the same night seemed to have no influence on my mother.

harness—a straitjacket as far as I was concerned—to which she attached a six-foot piece of line. Then she took me outside and set me down in the sand. At first I didn't understand what she wanted or expected me to do, so I just sat there looking up at her. After she took a step backwards and tugged on the line a couple of times I knew exactly what she had in mind. I'd seen enough dogs on leashes to get the picture. Well, she could forget it. It wasn't going to happen. I just sat there looking up at her. She tried verbal coaxing. Still, I just sat there. My father

25

tried his hand. When I refused to cooperate, he began dragging me along the ground like a pull toy. Well, I wasn't going to walk on a leash like some little slobbering, tail-wagging dog. I lay down on my side, figuring he would give up, but he continued to drag me through the sand for several feet before throwing down his end of the leash in exasperation. As he headed back toward the trailer I heard him mutter something that sounded like "stupid cat." Well, I had news for him, I wasn't stupid and I wasn't going to be leashed. He only tried

My mother was as determined to make me leash as is the postman to make his appointed rounds—weather did not deter either. My mother and I finally compromised. I would go wherever I wanted and she would follow me. In the end, she gave up and I regained my freedom.

one more time, but my mother seemed obsessed, trying time and time again. Sometimes we would sit and stare at each other, I at one end of the line and she at the other end. I still refused to leash like a little dog, but since being on the leash was my only chance to get outside the trailer, after a week or so we compromised. I would walk in whatever direction I desired, and she would follow.

The straitjacket served another purpose, which humiliated me even further. My father tied a long piece of shroud line to the harness and attached the other end to the Airstream. This, according to their theory, would allow me to exit and enter the trailer as I pleased and to spend as much time outside as I wanted, but would prevent me from running away or get-

26

ting lost. Get lost? Me? Never! I could spot our rig from a mile away, day or night, rain or shine. This stupid leash thing had to stop. I formulated a plan that was sure to drive them crazy. My objective, of course, was to rid myself of that ridiculous straitjacket and to regain my freedom and my dignity.

I sat by the door at night, wailing until my mother would strap me into the harness and tie me to the trailer. Once outside I would tangle the shroud line around whatever was available. A picnic table worked well. I would circle a leg on the table, jump over one bench, circle around another leg then jump over the other bench. Ten minutes of this and I would have the entire line wrapped around the table. Next I would begin caterwauling and pretend to choke. My father would then get out of bed, come outside and untangle me. I'd give him enough time to get back in bed before starting all over again. As the game continued, I found other ways of tangling the line. A combination of jumping over the Airstream's twin axles and working in and out through the tandem wheels was the most difficult to unravel. This required him to crawl underneath the trailer.

I took pride in my handiwork and became more creative as time went along. It took well over two months, and three states had slipped beneath the wheels of the Airstream before I finally prevailed. My mother gave up and put the straitjacket away. She placed a new collar around my neck with little chimes that tinkled when I moved, then opened the trailer door. I was now free to go and come as I pleased almost anytime we stopped.

Because we lived and traveled in a recreational vehicle we became known as "Fulltimers." I loved Fulltiming. I loved my newfound freedom, my new way of life and my new home on wheels. It would carry us almost anyplace we wanted to go and provided food, water, and shelter on the spot.

We parked our rig by roaring rivers, stayed in canyons with towering red sandstone mountains, camped in lush green forests by beautiful clear lakes, and sojourned in tranquil high mountain meadows with babbling brooks filled with trout. Strapped into the straitjacket I had been unable to fully enjoy all these new experiences, but now, free of all restraints, I explored everything to the fullest. I had never been happier.

27

We spent the larger part of the summer in the Rockies, the Tetons, and the Bitterroot. During that summer I observed numerous creatures of the wild and learned how they lived and what they did to survive. Some lived in trees, others lived underground, one family lived in a small cave with an underwater entrance, and another family I met, with long, broad, flat tails had built their house in the middle of a lake.

It was on a Sunday morning at Jackson Lake, Wyoming in Grand Teton National Park that we learned of the eruption of Mount Saint Helen's. The volcanic ash that settled on our picnic table sometime during the night had traveled on the wind for over five hundred miles. My mother promptly entered the event in her journal. She kept a day-to-day record of all the things we did and encountered during our travels.

These new experiences had a strange effect on me; visions of my ancient past flowed through my subconsciousness from time to time and I would entertain the notion that maybe I, too, could live in the wild. I knew I would never leave home. I knew also life for those living in the wilderness was a hard life of day-to-day survival and filled with uncertainty. Still, the thought, foolish as it was, lingered.

I learned early that not all wilderness people were friendly. I had several close calls during my travels, mostly forgotten now. None will ever eclipse that night in Death Valley, but another incident that first summer almost ended my travels before they got started. My first summer on the road could easily have been my last.

My parents were usually out during the day hiking, canoeing, fishing, taking pictures and that sort of thing, but the nighttime was my time. I loved the night and did most of my exploring by the light of the moon. In the early days I stuck pretty close to the Airstream, but as time passed I ventured farther and farther until one night I found myself lost. I had wandered around for over two hours trying to find some familiar scent or landmark. Soon, dawn would be breaking and I was beginning to panic.

My problems had begun when, following a very tasty and tender-looking baby rabbit, I failed to spot the coyote who was also stalking it. As I positioned myself for the attack I brushed one of my collar chimes against a clump of grass. In the midnight stillness of that small woodland meadow, the resultant tinkling sounded like a fire alarm. The rabbit bolted. I gave chase, but he dashed into one of several patches of blackberry vines and disappeared.

Having no desire to get cut up by the briers, I gave up well short of the thorny vines and was about to sit down when Mister Coyote decided to make his move. He was on top of me before I even knew he was there. My only option was to jump into the middle of the brier patch with the rabbit.

The coyote, not all that eager to get cut up by the thorns, slowly circled the blackberry vines, waiting for either me or the rabbit to try and escape. The rabbit, being more familiar with escape and evasion than I, was already in the next patch over. I had recovered somewhat; my heart was no longer in my throat, my pulse had returned to near normal, and I had regained most of my senses. I decided I would join the rabbit the first chance I got. If I could stick close to the rabbit, he might panic and break into the open, at which time the coyote would give chase and I would be able to escape back to the campground. This sort of game seemed natural for the rabbit. The coyote continued to circle the blackberry vines. I waited until he was on the opposite side of the berry patch, and then sprinted into the patch with the rabbit. The rabbit moved with lightning speed from one brier patch to another. Each time he moved, I followed.

29

Everything worked as planned, except for one small hitch. After switching brier patches a half dozen times, we ended up in a small patch with very few vines. The coyote took advantage of this and charged in after us. The rabbit broke cover with the coyote hot on his heels. I headed out in the opposite direction. When the rabbit escaped into another blackberry patch, the coyote wheeled and came after me. I was in the open and flat out of ideas so I fell back on the one strategy that had never let me down. A stand of lodgepole pines stood fifty feet away. If I could reach the trees I would be safe. The coyote was quick and in a matter of seconds had closed the distance until he was, literally, breathing down my back. Time had run out. Our final efforts were in sync, as though choreographed, but the coyote came up short. His teeth clicked shut on the empty air behind me as I hit the tree trunk a good six feet up. I had never leaped that high before. I didn't stop climbing until I reached the very top. It was a skinny tree and swayed back and forth under my weight, but I was safe and for the moment that was all that counted.

The coyote hung around for an hour or so, keeping a close eye on me while trying to sniff out the rabbit. I kept an even closer eye on him. He was sly and tried to bait me by pretending to leave and then circling around to watch me from behind a bush or brier patch. He must have figured I wasn't very bright. Maybe I wasn't, but I wasn't stupid either. I stayed in the tree two or three hours after he gave up and sauntered off for the last time.

A rain, starting as a light mist shortly after I took refuge in the tree had turned into a hard, steady downpour. I was cold, wet, hungry, and worst of all, lost. For the past few hours I had concentrated on surviving the jaws of death and had lost all sense of direction. While following the rabbit and trying to outwit the coyote, keeping up with where I was going or where I had been was the last thing on my mind. Normally I know where I am in relation to my little house and should it become necessary, which is rare, I can always sniff out my own trail back to familiar surroundings, but the rain had washed away my scent so there I was with no idea of which way to turn or in what direction my trailer was parked. I had already been wandering around trying to find some familiar

30

scent or landmark for more than two hours, dawn would be breaking soon, and I was beginning to panic when I spotted the Airstream at the "dump station."

Recreational vehicles are completely self-contained, providing all the luxuries of a stationary home. Recreational vehicles carry propane for cooking, heating, keeping the refrigerator cold, some even use propane for lighting. Batteries and generators provide electricity. They have a tank for carrying fresh water and other tanks to collect and hold waste water, but every few days it becomes necessary to resupply with fresh water and dump the holding tanks. Hence, the dump station.

Like in hotels, campers are normally required to check out before noon and since "RVers" usually stop at the dump station on their way out of the park, the line can get pretty long by midmorning. We had been in the park for over a week, so when I saw the Airstream at the dump station I assumed my parents were up early to beat the line and when finished would be heading back to the campground.

I jumped inside and was behind the couch in a flash and none too soon since the door slammed shut a couple of seconds later. I realized I had made a big mistake even before the bolt slid into place locking the door. Actually, to call it a big mistake would be seriously understating my predicament. Not spotting the coyote was a big mistake, this was a colossal mistake.

Although all Airstreams look pretty much the same, inside and out, I knew immediately I was in the wrong Airstream, but with the door closed and locked there was nothing I could do but wait. There was no way of knowing how far the owners of this Airstream would drive before they decided to stop and come inside. And then what? Were they nice people? Would they bring me back to the campground or would they throw me outside then drive away and leave me in a strange place with no idea of where to go or what to do?

Just when I thought things couldn't get any worse I heard him sniffing around. Couches in Airstreams are designed so the seat can slide forward allowing the back to fall flat, making an instant bed. The entire couch is built on a pedestal which sits about a foot away from the wall, but allows the

31

couch back to fit tight against the wall at all times. This provides plenty of room for my hidey-hole and lets me move about freely behind the couch. So, when the poodle stuck his head into my space, knowing he would easily fit behind the couch, I slipped out the opposite end.

I wasn't too concerned about the poodle. A swat across his face with my trusty right paw would no doubt open a couple of gashes in his nose and send him whining to his own secure corner of his trailer. But I needed time to think, so I leapt to the kitchen counter and watched him bounce up and down like a pogo stick. He looked more like a toy bouncing up and down than a dog; I guess that's why they're called toy poodles.

Poodles all have one thing in common—they are very noisy critters. This would work to my advantage, if all went as planned. Fulltimers are fairly predictable; just as stopping at the dump station is routine, so is stopping at the first available service station. This was part of my plan; I only hoped that first stop wouldn't be too far outside the park.

As we slowed down and turned off the road, inertia almost threw me off the counter and onto the poodle. My balancing act sent his yapping and bouncing-up-and-down routine into overdrive. I ignored the ruckus and concentrated on my plan. I heard a bell ring a couple of times as the driver eased his rig close to the gas pumps and came to a stop.

I hadn't realized before I began planning my escape that RVers are so predictable and disciplined; this insured my plan would work. Another habit of the RVer is to check inside the coach, at the first stop, to make sure everything is riding okay. Fulltimers always have a nagging suspicion, even after all the checking and double-checking, that they forgot to close a cabinet door or fasten the safety latch on the refrigerator or put something away. This fear of something left undone was the key to my plan. When the door opened—and I intended to make sure it did indeed open—I would make my escape.

The man got out of his Suburban tow vehicle, took a gas hose nozzle off its hook and began filling his tanks. The woman got out and headed straight for the trailer door, just as I knew she would. It was time to go into action. I wanted to make sure she opened the door in a hurry. I figured the best way to

32

accomplish this was to harass the poodle. I jumped from the counter onto the easy chair then onto the back of the couch. The poodle followed, yipping in a loud shrill voice. By running along the back of one couch, jumping to the second couch, then back to the kitchen counter, continuing around in a circle, I led him on a lively chase. The poodle followed, making so much noise anyone outside might easily have believed the poodle was being attacked by an alien from outer space. Just as the woman reached the door I quit playing ring-around-the-poodle and stopped on top of the kitchen counter. The poodle was bouncing up and down again and yipping louder than ever now that help was on its way. Just as the door opened I slapped the noisy little guy across his nose and my nails opened up a couple of nasty-looking gashes. He was probably more surprised than hurt, but he howled like I had struck a death blow and headed for the back of the trailer still yipping his head off. When the woman heard the poodle cry out in pain she yanked the door wide open. All she saw of me was a blur as I streaked past her and shot up a nearby tree. She let out a shriek, jumped out of my way and headed toward the back of the trailer where the poodle was cowering on the bed.

A couple of minutes later she rushed outside and began shouting, to her husband, that some mean renegade cat had stowed away inside the trailer and attacked her little Fluffy. She continued to complain about how I had almost killed her poor baby, all the while pointing an accusing finger in my direction.

By now, the sun had climbed well above the horizon and people were out moving about, going to work, school, shopping, and the like. The woman had leashed up the poodle and they were both under my tree yapping and pointing; she and the poodle had a lot in common. I wasn't paying much attention to them. I was too busy basking in the success of my well-executed escape, but a crowd soon gathered and, egged on by the woman and the poodle, began jabbering away and pointing at me. I was amused at first, but it wasn't long before I began to pick up a few disturbing words and phrases. *Rabies* was a word I heard bandied about, and the terms *pound* and *animal control* were repeated several times, but what really got my attention was a girl proudly proclaim-

33

ing, in a loud voice, that her boyfriend was on his way over with a shotgun. All things considered, I figured it was about time to bid these folks farewell. I climbed down to one of the lower branches and dropped onto a wood shed underneath the tree, leapt to the ground, and scrambled into the nearby woods. No one tried to stop me. No one came after me.

My problems, however, were a long way from over. I didn't know how far the poodle's parents had traveled before stopping or how long it would take me to get back to the campground, but I figured it would be simple enough to follow the road back to the park entrance. The road would lead through the park entrance straight on to the dump station, and somewhere past the dump station I would find the campground. A terrible thought raced across my consciousness. I had no idea how long it would take me to get back to the campground. If my journey took several days, would my parents conclude I had run away for sure this time and leave without me? I considered the possibility only momentarily before putting it out of my mind. They would wait. They would never leave without me; of this I was sure.

I worked my way back to the road and set out toward home. I kept to the tall grass at the edge of the road, which slowed my progress, but I was determined and kept a steady pace. I hadn't traveled for much over an hour before realizing I was tired and hungry. I had been up almost all night and had gone without food for most of that time. I must have been a throwback to a time when all my ancestors lived in trees because I loved trees. I felt safe high up in a tree. I found a tree to my liking and climbed onto a large limb bathed in warm rays of the midmorning sun. The limb concealed me from the prying eyes of any predator that might happen by and still gave me ample space to spread out and catch some badly needed Zs.

It was past noon and well past lunch before I awoke. Rested but still hungry I remained on my limb for a considerable time surveying the surroundings before finally spotting a family of mice living under a nearby stump. An elaborately built racetrack had been constructed just outside their front door. I've never understood why mice build racetracks and at the moment I really didn't care; the only thing important to me

34

was the fat little guy racing around the track stopping every so often to nibble on some grass or eat a fallen seed. When he was finally alerted to my presence, it was too late. I won't bore you with the details, but I will tell you he was quite tasty and I might add, very tender.

After lunch—actually, it was closer to tea time—I set out again in the direction of the park. By late afternoon I had covered a distance of just about two miles and was, once again, tired and hungry. I can survive a long time without food, weeks if necessary, although it would require restricting my activity to a minimum, but I can't survive the day without getting some sleep. When on the move I need both food and sleep to restore my energy; short naps, taken every few hours, are more in tune with my body chemistry than are longer periods of deep sleep. The late afternoon sun was warm and I dozed off quickly. When I awoke it was dark and had begun to mist again. I was still hungry, but hadn't been fortunate enough to stumble onto another mouse. I couldn't afford to take time out for serious hunting— time was precious. I knew my parents would wait as long as they could; however, the choice might not be theirs to make. In many state parks and forest service campgrounds there is no time limit for camping, but this was a high-use park and the ranger limited campers to a maximum stay of fourteen days. We were nearing the end of our second week and I doubted the ranger would extend our stay just because of a lost cat. He was very strict about keeping pets on a leash and would probably delight in the notion of a big-city cat lost in the woods. If my parents were forced to leave the park without me I might never see them again. The thought was troubling and disheartening.

Dawn was breaking when I finally reached the park. The sight of the entrance station was a great relief; it meant I was better than halfway home, providing my home was still there. The ranger's house was a couple of hundred yards past the entrance station and sat back about fifty yards off the road. He must have been an early riser because the smell of frying bacon wafted out to the road, beckoning me. I knew hanging around the ranger's door would only get me into more trouble, but I thought, just possibly, there

35

might be something in his garbage can to tide me over until I could rustle up something on my own—a mistake that only succeeded in slowing me down. The ranger had a log house and a large yard surrounded by a rail fence made of split cedar. I sprang to the top rail with ease, and sat motionless for a few moments surveying the area in back of his house. Sure enough, a couple of large garbage cans stood near the garage, their lids ajar. I was about halfway to the trash cans when I first heard him. Had I been more alert I would have retreated immediately, but fatigue and hunger clouded my thinking and I stopped for a moment to locate and identify the source of the muffled sound. That moment of indecision almost cost me my life. He came tearing out of his house near the ranger's back door and headed straight across the yard towards me. I reached the fence barely a heartbeat ahead of the big German shepherd. As I cleared the fence, I heard him throw his weight hard against the split cedar. I stopped twenty or thirty feet away, in the first available tree, and looked back. He was still leaning against the fence with his head hanging over the top railing, watching me. Well, I wasn't going to get anything to eat at the ranger's house, so I figured I might as well take advantage of the tree, since I had already climbed it, catch a few winks, and hope for something to eat later on.

It was midmorning before I climbed down and walked back to the road. The sky had cleared and the sun's rays probing through the trees warmed me and drove the chill from my bones as it dried my rain-soaked fur. Although hungry, I felt better than I had at any time since my ordeal began. With a steady pace I reached the dump station by early afternoon. I was on my way home!

Nearby stood a big dumpster where campers leaving the park deposited their garbage. Sometimes, in order to lighten their load or in the case of "weekenders" not wanting to carry extra food home, they throw away some pretty tasty goodies. The lid was open and it wouldn't take much time to check it out, so why not, I might get lucky. One good leap would put me on top of the dumpster and from there I could check out its contents. I don't know if it was carelessness, or fatigue, or perhaps I was just a bit weak from hunger—whatever the

36

case might be, I misjudged and sailed over the top, landing not only in the middle of all the trash inside, but on top of another guy looking for an easy meal. He had been dining on some discarded fish parts when I so unceremoniously dropped in and most likely figured I intended to steal his lunch. Needless to say, he was upset.

He didn't outweigh me by much, but had that lean and wiry look. I knew at a glance I didn't want to mess around with this guy. He looked like he knew how to handle himself in any situation. He had already made it quite clear he had no intention of sharing his food. An apology would be a waste of time. Exiting in one giant leap I hit the ground running without ever looking back. Luckily, my hasty departure had carried me in the direction of the campground.

I continued without even realizing I was walking in the middle of the road, my mind on all the comforts and good food awaiting me at home. Although preoccupied, I still had my senses about me and when I saw the shadow racing along the ground toward me I headed for cover.

Instinct had triggered my action, but I knew I was in the land of the golden eagle and a tree would provide no protection from a skyborne hunter. I raced toward a nearby thicket and disappeared into the dense undergrowth in the nick of time, as his wings fluttered just above my head.

Once my heart slowed down I chanced a quick look outside the thicket; he was still there, circling effortlessly overhead. He could probably see me quite easily. The term *eagle eyes* probably wasn't coined without justification. My only choice was to keep out of sight until he got tired of waiting and cruised on to another potential meal. If I ever got home, I would never go outside again!

With no place to go until Mister Eagle cleared out, I figured I might as well take another nap. I slipped underneath a fallen tree overgrown with brambles, found a nice soft spot, lay down and closed my eyes.

When I awoke I eased from my hiding place and peered outside the thicket. A full moon hanging in a star-studded sky painted everything with a silvery glow. Traveling should be easy. By now, however, the lack of food was taking its toll. I was getting weak and my nerves were shot. I jumped at ev-

37

ery shadow and every leaf that rustled in the gentle winds on this soft summer evening.

I stopped dead in my tracks. What was it? I opened my mouth, extended my tongue and tasted the air. My pulse quickened, but not because I was frightened. It was jubilation that increased my heart rate.

Drifting on the breeze was a familiar aroma—the smell of food cooking over an open fire. This could mean only one thing; campers were nearby. Fifteen minutes later I could see campfires glowing in the distance. Suddenly, with the delicious aroma of fresh trout cooking over an open fire filling my nostrils, I found new strength that carried me faster and faster toward the circle of scattered fires.

I spotted my trailer exactly where I had left it, and with a newfound strength that added extra spring to my step I closed the distance in a matter of seconds. My mother was arranging bowls of food on our picnic table. Two plates were set, complete with place mats, flatware, and cloth napkins. My father loathed paper napkins. I can hear him now, "Paper napkins are a communist plot."

He had just transferred two sixteen-inch rainbow trout from the grill above the campfire to a serving platter and was carefully stacking hot cornbread pancakes, made from a secret recipe or so he claimed, on the platter with the trout when I casually strolled into camp. I wanted to leap into my mother's arms and tell her how much I had missed her. I wanted to tell her how much I had worried that I might never see her again. I wanted to tell her how tired and hungry I was and how scared I had been. I wanted to tell her all these things and more, but pride got in my way. So, flaunting my independence and self-confidence, I greeted my parents casually, as usual, continued at a leisurely gait to the picnic table, jumped up on the nearest bench, and began begging for food. Begging for food was to be expected. I did it at every meal. I acted as if nothing unusual had happened and didn't care whether they gave me food or not, although at that moment I would have traded my soul for a piece of trout and a cornbread pancake.

My mother's head snapped around when she heard my greeting and in a chastising but emotional voice she asked,

38

"Where have you been, young lady?" She rushed over, picked me up, hugged me and buried her face in my fur.

"Don't you know I've been worried sick about you?" I watched as tears formed in my mother's eyes. Had she looked closely she would have seen tears in my eyes, as well. It was good to be home, I was very happy, very happy indeed.

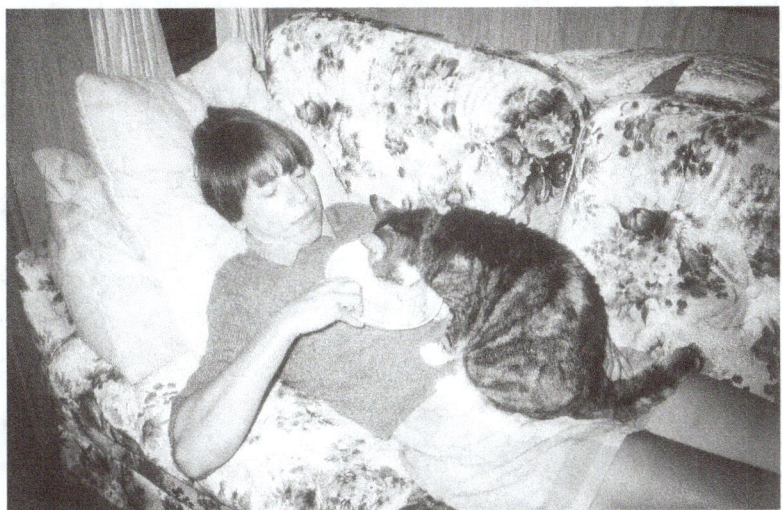

I always tried to finagle a bite of whatever my parents were eating and I was usually successful. Most of the things they ate were very good, but occasionally they ate really strange stuff that smelled terrible and tasted even worse. I often wondered why such food didn't make them sick.

40

Chapter IV
Nowhere To Run

Growing up in Bonita I was unaware of seasons. The temperature changed a few degrees from time to time, but I never considered it winter or summer, or spring or fall. There was sunshine just about every day, flowers bloomed continually, and leaves were always green. Every day and everything was pretty much the same. But now, there were changes every minute, or so it seemed.

At first, changes were subtle. The warm afternoons lingered as the sun hung stubbornly in the western sky as if trying to defy the natural order of things. But, unable to do so, it sank ever so slowly beyond the horizon, setting the lazily drifting puffer bellies ablaze. Alpenglow playing along the mountaintops ushered in the evening. The delicate aroma of night-blooming flowers wafted on gentle breezes that rippled the tall grass and rustled leaves in the big cottonwoods around the lake where we camped and along the streams that fed the lake.

My parents took full advantage of these warm days they called Indian Summer by hiking, canoeing, and fishing; my father loved to fish. We ate trout every day. He caught fish where other people swore there weren't any. As for me, I explored at night, becoming more and more familiar with the wilderness around me. During the day I enjoyed the panorama outside my windows from the back of the couch and as warm rays of the afternoon sun soaked my fur I would

We camped in every environment imaginable—in the searing heat of the desert, in canyons so deep the sun never touched us, in high mountain meadows carpeted with wildflowers, by lakes where we were sometimes dusted with an early snow, and by streams where my father caught trout. Here at Slough Creek in Yellowstone National Park, Wyoming, my father caught trout right in front of the Airstream and cooked them over the campfire.

doze and dream of life in the wilds. Sometimes visions of creatures unfamiliar, yet not unlike myself, possibly my ancestors from a time long ago, would drift through my dreams.

The warm days passed quickly. With each journey the sun made across the sky its path became shorter as it moved closer to the southern horizon. As the sun's path shortened so did the days, and as the days shortened the nights became longer and cooler. Soon the night wind carried a chill that sometimes brought an involuntary shiver. Dew that formed

42

in the wee morning hours would, by dawn, turn into tiny white crystals that crunched under my paws.

Each new day brought more changes. Summer's soft green grass turned to various shades of brown, rust, and amber. Flowers bowed their heads and shed their petals—seeds scattered on the breeze, assuring their perpetuity. Birch and aspen dotting the meadow and stretching up the mountain slopes were a kaleidoscope of color. Each gust of wind, no

Here at Bryce Canyon, Utah I experienced my first snowfall. We were camped on the canyon rim at an elevation above 8,000 feet and were surprised by a late spring snow. At first I didn't know what to make of it, but decided that I didn't like it very much. It was much later with many snowfalls having come and gone that I came to appreciate the white fluffy stuff.

longer warm and gentle, unloosed a golden shower from the nearby cottonwoods.

Songbirds had departed for warmer climates. Other inhabitants of the forest, either preferring to stay or unable to leave, were busy preparing for the impending winter when temperatures would drop well below freezing and no one would dare venture outside. They toiled with an apparent sense of urgency during these short days, collecting and storing food. Mice, voles, and shrews searched for grass seed; squirrels cut and stored pine cones; even the beaver family worked with a

43

greater fervor carrying freshly cut branches across the lake to their lodge. I envied these creatures of the wild their independence and freedom.

I sat watching the awesome sight of Canada geese in their familiar V, sweeping southward across the moon, their eerie honking a reminder that winter was close at hand, and pondered my chances of surviving the winter on my own. I was dependent upon my parents and without them would in all likelihood perish. I found this unsettling. Why should this disturb me? Was there some ancient call of the wild, a genetic code buried deep within my brain that I could not possibly understand? Had my travels of the last few months triggered this code? Was this responsible for my strange dreams? I put it all out of my mind. It didn't matter. I would never leave my parents and they would never abandon me.

There was a new chill in the air. Little clouds formed in front of my face each time I exhaled, and tiny ice crystals collected on my whiskers. Hunting was poor. The fat field mice were now content to spend the nights in their underground homes. They would wait for the morning sun's warm rays to drive away the chill before venturing out in search of the few remaining grass seeds; any seeds they were fortunate enough to find would be added to their winter storehouse. I sat patiently by the front door of a very plump little guy whose skills in escape and evasion had been more than a match for my own cunningness. I had waited for over an hour and knew it highly unlikely he would leave his well-sheltered and comfortable little abode before morning. Still, I sat and waited. Catching him would do a lot more for my ego than for my stomach. I knew he was home by the mousebreath outside his front door. Water vapor escaping as he breathed had collected on the withered brown grass that concealed the entrance to his cozy, and no doubt, well-stocked burrow. In the cold, dry night air it had crystallized into hoarfrost. By the amount of mousebreath present I suspected he had been home all night.

The Airstream's water pump gave me a start. I was a considerable distance from our trailer, but in the early morning stillness it sounded like a jackhammer. The water pump was a signal my mother was up and making coffee. She routinely

44

rose before dawn. After a cup of coffee and a bagel, or some-times a bran muffin, she did stretching exercises. Then, just as dawn was breaking, she would begin her morning run. I normally went home at this time, spent a little time with her, ate breakfast, and went to bed. So, upon hearing the water pump I gave up my quest and headed for home. The mouse had unknowingly received a reprieve; he would live to see another sunrise.

As I was about to leap over a small stream that ran into the lake just a few feet behind our trailer, I noticed the water wasn't moving. This was strange. I had taken a drink from the stream only a few hours ago. I decided to climb down the bank and investigate. I could hear the bubbling, gurgling sound of running water, but the water wasn't moving. I touched it with my paw and to my amazement found it solid. When I licked the hard shiny water I found it very cold and my tongue almost stuck to the surface. I then realized it was ice, just like the kind that comes out of the refrigerator. It wasn't in little cubes, but it was ice, nevertheless. Still contemplating the frozen stream, I put my other front paw on the ice. When nothing happened I decided to walk across. As I neared the opposite side I elected to leap onto the bank, rather than climb the steep three-foot incline. I unleashed the power in my haunches, but instead of propelling myself onto the bank above, my rear legs broke through the ice with a splashing, crunching sound. I tried leaping again, but this time my front legs broke through the stream's frozen surface. I tried leaping to the other side a third time, but only succeeded in making splashing sounds. I struggled frantically, but to no avail. My paws had punched holes in the ice, but because my stomach still rested on the stream's frozen surface, my legs did not reach the bottom and there was nothing for me to push against; I was stuck. The cold water underneath the ice instantly soaked through my fur and reached my skin with immediate bone-chilling effect. I could no longer make my legs move and the numbing cold was spreading through the rest of my body. I realized if I remained in the frozen stream I would die, but I was helpless to free myself. My mother was my only hope. I cried out as loud as I could and prayed she would hear me. When the trailer door opened I began crying even more loudly, if that were possible. I could hear my mother's footsteps approaching, but I continued crying until she knelt down, grabbed me by the nape of the neck and pulled me from the icy water.

Perhaps it went back to the time I ran away or the time I got lost and didn't return home for two days—whatever the reason, when we arrived at a new place my mother took me outside and we had a little talk about being careful and not getting lost.

She pressed me to her breast, hurried inside, turned up the furnace and while holding me in the stream of warm air flowing from the heater vent, began toweling me dry. My father, awakened by the unusual activity, sat up in bed and learning

46

of my mishap began harassing me, as was to be expected. Looking me directly in the eye, he asked, "How old are you now?" He paused for a moment, and then continued as though I had answered his question. "How did you get to be so dumb in such a short time?" I turned my head and looked away as though embarrassed. I would have been hurt had I thought he was serious, but I knew he wasn't. It was a game we played. He would tell me how dumb and ugly I was and

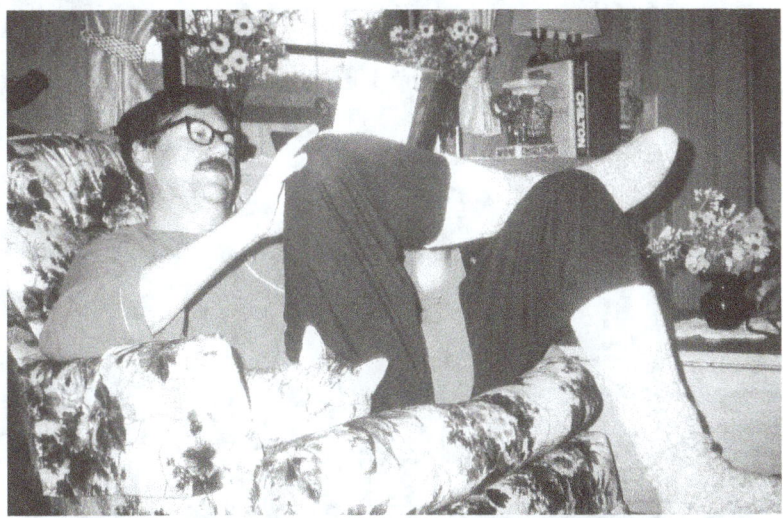

It always mystified me why, with the Royals being so roomy and having so many places to sit, my father had to sit in my chair. Actually I loved the attention I got when he sat down. He'd gently move me over to one side and ease into the chair, then after a few minutes I'd climb onto his lap and he talked to me while stroking my fur and scratching my chin.

I would pretend not to like him, but I sat on his lap at every opportunity and each time he would rub my head, scratch my chin, and stroke my fur. Sometimes while in his lap I would fall asleep. He loved me as much as I loved him. Anytime I was in danger he would come to my rescue, often at his own peril.

I remember a day back in Bonita when Harley, a big mean guy who didn't seem to like anyone very much, chased me home. Yelling as loudly as I could I headed for the garage where I knew my father was working. As I streaked through the open door and onto a workbench, with Harley hot on my heels, my father grabbed him by the tail. Harley turned on my father, laying his forearm open in several places with his sharp claws. When the incident was over my father surveyed his wounds, looked down at me and said, "You sure hang out with a rough crowd." He then smiled at me and added, "You big dummy."

My mother finished her coffee and went off on her morning run. I headed for my food dish. My father made himself a cup of hot tea, sweetened it with cream and honey, rearranged the pillows and leaned back to watch the sunrise.

My parents loved the outdoors and loved hiking; here they can be seen on the south rim of Zion Canyon in Utah. I can't begin to imagine how long it took the Virgin River, a very small stream, to carve out such a magnificent monument to nature. I also wonder how long it took my parents to get up there, since we were camped on the canyon floor.

After I finished eating I leapt onto his lap and as he sipped his tea and stroked my fur I fell asleep, purring my contentment. I was undisturbed when, after finishing his tea, my father moved me off his lap onto the bed, got dressed, and went outside.

It was midmorning before I awoke. After my wake-up stretch and a few Purina Stars I headed for my lookout perch, but

48

finding the door open I ventured outside instead. I was surprised to find the canoe tied down on top of the El Camino. Inspecting further I found all our gear stowed, the fire ring cleaned and raked, and the El Camino hooked up to the Airstream. This could mean only one thing: we were breaking camp. I wondered where we were going and what new adventure awaited me. Just thinking about a new place to explore was always exciting.

My mother was busy arranging things inside the El Camino while my father studied a road atlas which lay open on the hood. He flipped the pages back and forth, checking some in

When in the Lower 48, we didn't always stay in commercial camper parks; perhaps I exaggerate that from time to time. After a day of backpacking in Glacier National Park, Montana, my parents set up their tent in the designated area—permits are required for backcountry camping in the park—they awoke the next morning to find themselves camping with a family of goats.

detail while only glancing at others. Finally he closed the atlas and said, "We should be in San Diego by the end of the week with time to spare."

What did he say? San Diego! Why San Diego? I thought about it for a minute or so and I didn't like what I was thinking. Were we moving back to Bonita? Surely not! Why would anyone

49

want to live in the city where traffic noise never ceased, where it never got dark because the street lights are never extinguished and the air is so polluted you can't smell the flowers? Why couldn't we continue to live the way we were living now? Don't misunderstand—I was very lucky to have grown up in Bonita and I have lots of good memories from my kittenhood, but now I would be bored to death living in a house that stood still, a house that never moved, a house that stayed in one place forever. But what could I do? I had no choice. If my parents were going back to Bonita, I would have to go also. And then again, maybe not, maybe I did have a choice. I could just stay right here in this little meadow. But how would I survive? Too many questions. I needed time to think.

I headed down towards the lake where a thicket grew along the shoreline, but had gone only a short distance when I heard my father say, "Well, guess we're about ready. Is everything in the trailer okay?"

"I believe so." my mother replied, then added, "Make sure Honeybee is inside before you lock the door." They were ready to leave. What was I going to do?

"She's not in here," he called out.

"You'd better find her," she called back.

He spotted me almost immediately upon exiting the Airstream and said, "Okay Bee, inside."

I just stood looking at him. He started walking toward me; I knew he intended to pick me up, carry me to the trailer and lock me inside. Well, he could forget it, I had made up my mind, I wasn't going anywhere. I was staying right here. I waited until he was within a few feet of me, then headed full speed for my secret hiding place in the thicket. He followed, taking his time, while muttering something about how I was the dumbest cat he'd ever seen and how I was getting dumber every day. When he reached the thicket he started talking to me as though he knew exactly where I was hiding. Fat chance.

"You'd better get in the house," when talking to me about the Airstream, he always referred to it as *the house*, "or we'll leave without you, you little varmint." My thoughts were, "Well go ahead, see if I care." He bent over, picked up a stick, and began beating the bushes as he walked along the edge of the thicket.

50

"Okay, I'm tired of fooling around, you'd better get in the house, if you know what's good for you." He walked a little farther, beat on a few more bushes and said, "Alright, stay out here, starve and freeze, see if I care, you big dummy."

He was right, as much as I resented it, I knew I couldn't survive by myself. I had known it all along. I was just disappointed at the thought of giving up my new life and moving back into a house where you always saw the same thing every time you looked out the window, day after day, year in, year out. I waited until he was several feet past my hiding place before heading for the trailer. Leaves crunching underneath my feet alerted him to the fact that I had vacated my hiding place. As I streaked for the trailer he thrashed the ground with his stick and yelled, "You'd better run, you ugly little varmint."

This was the beginning of a new game. Anytime my parents wanted me inside, for any reason whatsoever, I would hide. My father then came looking for me, yelling, throwing twigs in the direction of my suspected hiding place—either he never knew where I was hiding or he intentionally threw them in the wrong direction. Whenever I broke cover he beat the ground with a stick and yelled even louder. Just as a football player sometimes shows off crossing the goal line by slowing to a walk when he knows the defender has no chance of catching him I, too, would slow to a walk just before reaching the trailer. We both knew he couldn't catch me unless I let him.

For almost a month we had camped by a long narrow lake which lay across the U.S.-Canadian border. The lake could only be reached by a dirt road, full of chuckholes and washboards, that wound and twisted its way for fifty miles through the mountains. The road was narrow, treacherous, and slow going. Even with a midmorning start it was well into the afternoon before we reached pavement.

Forty-five minutes later we stopped for gasoline in a small town at the junction of a major highway. This junction marked the beginning of our journey towards the most southwest corner of the country. My parents were unhurried in their preparations for the long trip. After gassing up the El Camino, filling the Airstream's propane tanks and buying groceries,

51

they prepared and ate lunch before getting underway. I wasn't hungry. My stomach was empty, but I just didn't have an appetite, so I stayed behind the couch trying not to think about returning to what was sure to be a boring life in Bonita.

I abandoned my favorite spot on back of the front couch and spent most of the next five days in my hidey-hole. I wondered if I would be able to readjust to city life. After the last six months I could never again be content with the little acre I had loved so much in my youth. Knowing I would still be with my parents was my only solace.

There were ways I could tell, whenever we stopped, if our stay would be a few minutes, a few hours, or several days. When my father began leveling the trailer I knew, even without leaving my hidey-hole, we had reached our destination. The sad day had arrived. Life on the road had come to an end. The adventures of Fulltiming had been reduced to memories.

Shortly after arriving my parents showered, changed clothes, and drove away in the El Camino. I decided to take a look outside and see what, if anything, had changed in the old neighborhood. I wondered if Butch was still around. I dragged myself out of my hidey-hole and with a sigh and a halfhearted leap reached the back of the couch. I looked outside and couldn't believe my eyes. We were in a commercial RV park. We rarely stayed in commercial parks, which suited me just fine. I preferred backcountry campgrounds. So, where were we? I was confused. Why weren't we in Bonita?

The unmistakable odor of salt and fish drifted through the open window. I remembered the aroma from the short time I'd lived with my biological mother in Coronado and knew we were near the ocean. This only served to further confuse me.

My parents returned late and went straight to bed. I had been unable to get past them when they opened the door since they were alert to all my old tricks. My sit-by-the-door-and-complain routine had no chance of working since they were asleep before I had time to get on their nerves. Every day for the next week they left by midmorning and did not return until well after dark. Twice they did not come home until the following night. Their routine had provided no opportunity for me to get outside and I was getting tired of being cooped up all the time. I was about ready to start climb-

52

ing the walls when to my surprise, they slept late and spent all day at home. I was determined to get outside, one way or another, and this was going to be the day, but I knew I had to make it happen.

I stayed close to the door all afternoon, hoping they would get careless when entering or exiting and I would be able to

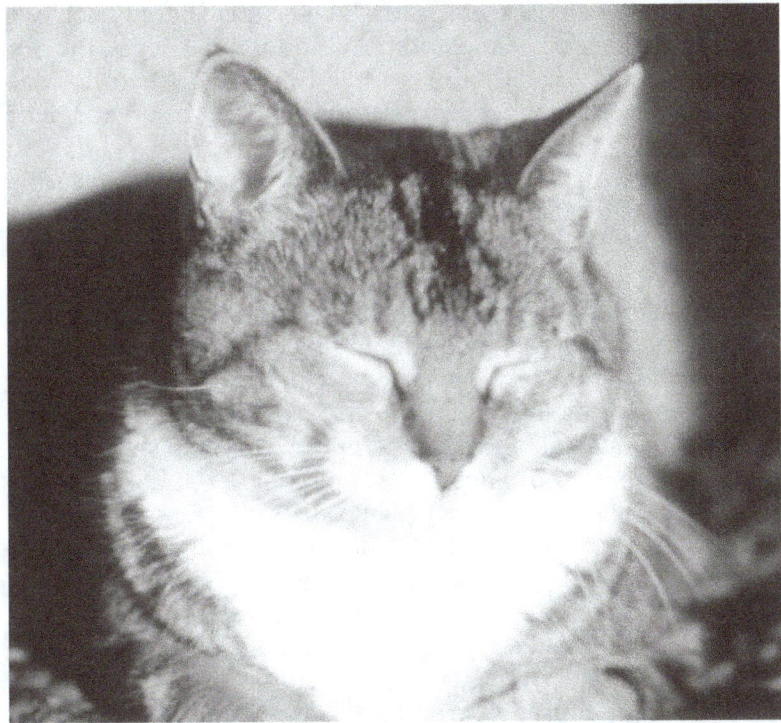

During the day my parents usually left me alone inside the Airstream while they were outside pursuing their own interests. I didn't mind—the nighttime was my time and while they were gone I dozed in my father's chair or slept on the back of the couch.

slip past them, but I was unsuccessful. The sun was just sinking below the horizon when I went into my act. I sat by the door and looked first at one of my parents and then the other while crying as pitifully as I possibly could. It took over an hour, but it paid off, as I knew it would. It always did. Unable to listen to any more of my moaning, my mother got up and opened the door. I was outside and under the trailer in a flash.

53

With so many streetlights it was difficult to tell exactly when twilight gave way to darkness. Even so, there were plenty of shadows to conceal my movements. I worked my way to the perimeter of the park and found myself on a narrow beach. I walked along the beach and discovered the RV park to be at the end of a narrow peninsula that stuck out into what I would later learn was Mission Bay—a place to which we would return many times when visiting San Diego. But for the time being everything was still a mystery. I had no idea where we were or what purpose our being here served. Since I hadn't been outside for a week I decided to enjoy the night rather than worry about things I couldn't change. So, clearing my mind of all misgivings, I set out on a leisurely stroll to see what I could find of interest.

By midnight I had familiarized myself with the entire park, except for one area, an area I had purposely saved for last. Behind the office was an intriguing plot about the size of my old backyard in Bonita. This is where the manager kept all his equipment for maintaining the park. Near a gate that opened out onto the street stood a big dumpster. An open shed ran the entire length of the fence on the park side. Underneath the shed were flats of bedding plants, flats of grass, flowers in pots, a few small trees in big containers and all sorts of other interesting-looking stuff. Vegetables grew along the back fence. This looked like a good place to rustle up a fat, unsuspecting mouse. I hadn't eaten in well over six hours and I was ready for a snack. Ready? I was way past ready.

An hour of hunting turned up only a couple of lizards. Lizards, yuck! I was hungry but not desperate. The junk piles also proved fruitless. Well, there was always the dumpster. Occasionally a really tasty treat can be found in a dumpster. As I padded toward the dumpster the smell of fried chicken caught my attention. I followed the tantalizing aroma to a box made of heavy wire mesh. The box was open at one end. At the far end of the box, opposite the opening were a couple of chicken wings. Something about the box struck me as odd, but I didn't know what. I walked around the box a couple of times and still couldn't figure it out. Actually, everything about the box was strange. Why would anyone go to all the trouble of hiding food in a box without a door? It

54

didn't make any sense. Oh well, finders keepers, losers weepers. The chicken smelled delicious. I could hardly wait to bite into one of the wings, but I didn't like the idea of dining inside the wire box. If the owner of the chicken wings returned it wasn't likely a thief in the night would be well received, so I decided to take the chicken outside. Underneath one of the tractors would be a fitting place to eat this unexpected, mouth-watering treat. I entered the box and took both wings firmly between my teeth. Intending to exit the box as quickly as I had entered I turned to leave, but found a string holding the chicken wings to the bottom of the wire box. I tightened my jaws and gave it a good yank. There was a barely audible click as the string came loose. Simultaneously, at the open end a loud clanging noise caused me to jump and hit my head on the top of the box. Without any thought as to what might have happened, I whirled toward the opening intending to flee, but instead, stood motionless. There was nowhere to run! The end of the box that had been open only a heartbeat earlier was now blocked by a steel door. I was trapped!

In panic, I tore at the wire mesh with my teeth until my mouth was bleeding. I accomplished nothing as the wire held tight, unyielding. As the panic subsided and my heart rate returned to normal I began to appraise my situation. It wasn't good. My parents were too far away to hear me no matter how loudly I wailed. It would be a total waste of energy. There was nothing to do but wait. Wait for what?

I knew if I did not return home before my mother left on her warm-up walk, a prelude to her morning run, she would come looking for me. If I hadn't returned home by the time she finished her run, she would send my father out to search for me—it had become my father's duty to investigate whenever I stayed away too long. He accepted this duty, I believe, not only to please my mother but because he, too, worried about me. I consoled myself knowing my parents loved me and would leave no stone unturned in their efforts to find me. I was reminded once again how much I depended on my parents and, as always, I found this disturbing.

Time passed slowly. It seemed like an eternity before the first hint of dawn. I could not tell when the stars first began to

55

fade, but soon all but the brightest had disappeared and gray bands of light were forming above the eastern horizon. Songbirds struck up their morning chorus and a few people were getting up and moving about. I knew my mother was one of those people and she would be looking for me at this very moment. I listened to every footstep, hoping to recognize hers so that I might call out to her, but it didn't happen. All kinds of people passed near enough to be heard, but she wasn't one of them. The sun climbed slowly through a few lazily drifting white clouds into a blue California sky, promising another beautiful day. A beautiful day for everyone but me. My day promised gloom and despair. I tried to stay awake and alert, but having stayed up most of the night I dozed off. I awoke to the sound of approaching footsteps. When they stopped I looked up at a heavyset woman peering in at me.

"Uh huh," she grunted, turned and walked away. I listened to her footsteps as they faded and somewhere in the distance a door slammed shut. Then all was quiet. I went back to sleep.

Somewhere around noon, judging from the sun, I was awakened again by footsteps I recognized as belonging to the heavyset lady. Two other sets of footsteps accompanied her. My spirits soared; she had found my parents. My jubilation was short lived when I realized the footsteps did not belong to my parents. The two new people, a man and a woman, were in uniform. The man carried a smaller, but similar, version of the cage that held me prisoner. The man, a gruff little guy, knelt down and peered through the wire at me for ten or fifteen seconds before pulling on a pair of heavy gloves that extended all the way to his elbows. While mumbling something under his breath, which didn't sound very nice, he opened a trapdoor in the top of my cage, reached in with one hand and grabbed me by the nape of the neck. I spat, hissed, and tried to scratch and bite him, but the heavy gloves protected him. He retaliated by shoving my face into a corner and pinning my body to the bottom of the cage. I continued to squirm, trying to get at him with my teeth and claws for a few more seconds before giving up. I reasoned that if I continued to resist he might really hurt me. So far he had been firm but not abusive. When I gave up the fight and relaxed, he lifted me out and gently deposited me inside the smaller

56

cage. After a brief conversation with the heavyset woman the man picked up his cage and followed by the lady in uniform, carried me to a truck parked in front of the office. As we approached the truck my heart sank even lower, if that was possible. The sign on the truck's door read, San Diego County Animal control.

I wasn't alone in the back of the truck. It was filled with cages just like mine. Most were empty, but a few sad-looking faces peered out at me from their wire prisons. For the rest of the afternoon we cruised around residential neighborhoods, stopping occasionally to apprehend other unsuspecting criminals. I wondered if their crimes were worse than mine. I knew stealing was wrong, but I never realized taking two chicken wings could land me in jail. By the end of the day when we arrived at the animal shelter only a couple of cages were unoccupied.

The driver parked the truck inside a covered compound where one by one we were placed in larger and sturdier cages built along the compound's perimeter. The wire mesh floors of the new cages where uncomfortable to walk, stand, sit or even lie on; I was getting really tired of wire mesh. Dinky metal containers fastened to the inside of the doors served as food and water bowls, a reminder I hadn't eaten in almost twenty-four hours. I wished, now, that I had eaten the chicken wings. I shouldn't have passed up a chance to eat, especially after going without food for so long and having no idea when I would eat again, but when the trap sprang shut I lost my appetite. Now I was starving. When the food and water finally arrived, I ate every morsel and lapped every drop. Then, tired, lonely, and scared I lay down and went to sleep.

Somewhere around midmorning another uniformed man came through, refilling food and water dishes. As he approached my cage he asked, "How are you feeling this morning young lady?" He seemed nice enough, even sincere, but when he asked, "Did you have a restful night?" I began to suspect he was being facetious. I really didn't care one way or the other. I had too many things on my mind to be concerned about the man's personality. I was still hungry, so when he started filling my bowl I stood up and stretched, eager to get at the food. When the man heard my collar chimes

57

tinkling he peered into my cage for a closer look and asked, "Well now, pretty lady, what's that you have around your neck?" He continued talking to me while filling my food and water containers. I ignored him and waited until he moved to another cage before approaching the food. I had finished eating and must have been napping since I wasn't aware the man had returned and was standing in front of my cage until I heard his voice. "Well Missy, let's see what secrets you're hiding underneath that long fur of yours."

When he opened the door and I saw the heavy elbow-length glove on his left hand I knew what to expect and didn't resist. I had learned struggling accomplished nothing except to insure my face would be shoved into the corner of the cage. He grabbed me by the nape of the neck with the gloved hand and held me firmly against the floor while with his other hand he loosened and removed my collar. He closed the door, stood back and after inspecting my collar, said, "Well young lady, I see you have a name." He leaned down and stared at me for few seconds then exclaimed, "I guess you do look a little bit like a honeybee." With that he stood up, walked across the compound and disappeared into a building by the big front gate.

My second day in jail dragged by even more slowly than the first, which only yesterday had seemed impossible. Except for conversations with nearby prisoners, there was nothing to do except eat, sleep, and worry. These conversations were very depressing, so I tried putting them out of my mind, but I couldn't. The story was always the same and although it was apparent some of the new inmates repeated only what they had heard, most knew firsthand what happened to long-term prisoners. Very few, according to the old-timers, were ever bailed out. All others, after a while, just disappeared, never to be seen or heard from again. I knew my parents would come and get me, but I was saddened just knowing many of the prisoners had no one to come for them and would eventually just disappear as if they had never existed.

As the days passed I resigned myself to eating, sleeping, and waiting. I awoke one morning and unable to recall how many days had passed since my capture, realized I had lost all track of time. Unsettling thoughts began to form in the back of my mind and flowed to the surface as disturbing questions. Where were my parents? Why hadn't they come for me? Had they been unable to find me and given up the search? Did they think I had run away again and hadn't bothered to look for me, waiting for me to come home on my own? Would they ever come?

I became more and more paranoid as the days crept by until emotion, not logic ruled my thinking. When I awoke to find the cage next door empty, where only yesterday Fat Foot (so named because of the six toes on each of her front paws) had resided, I no longer doubted the stories about disappearing inmates.

As the man who had been feeding me approached I thought he was bringing more food and water, but as he drew closer I noticed the boxlike container he carried in his right hand. The container was made of green plastic, had several small holes in each side and wasn't much larger than a couple of shoe boxes stacked on top of one another. It reminded me of the ugly plastic toys one often finds in backyards, always strewn about in an unsightly mess. The handle on top allowed him to carry it much the same as you would carry an attaché case. He opened my cage and wearing the same heavy gloves I'd become accustomed to seeing, grabbed me by the nape of the neck and transferred me to the plastic box. It was very small. Once inside I could barely turn around. When he was sure the door to the box was closed and the latch fastened, he picked me up and started walking toward the building near the front gate. Where was he taking me? Why wasn't he talking to me as he usually did? It came to me in a rush. I was panicked, but there was nothing I could do. I hadn't bothered to count days; it had seemed unimportant. I had kept telling myself my parents would come and rescue me, but it hadn't happened and now my time was up. I started to cry. When I began crying the man lifted me up, peered through the peephole and said, "Don't worry, it'll all be over soon." Those words, left no doubt in my mind; my time was up and I was going to disappear.

I knew neither the man nor time had slowed down. I knew it was an illusion. But I didn't know it was the extra adrenaline flowing through my veins which enabled my brain to process everything at warp speed that gave the appearance of slow motion. During this interval of apparent slow motion every action and every detail was etched indelibly in my mind. The man walked across the compound, opened a door, and continued down a passageway for a short distance before entering a well-lighted office. He put me down on a chair in front of the only desk in the room. The desk was littered with notepads, forms of all kinds, newspapers, clipboards, magazines and all sorts of other stuff. He bent over and began stirring things around on top of the desk. After several seconds of moving stuff from one spot to another he stopped and grasped something in his right hand. As he straightened up and shifted the item to his left hand I heard the familiar tinkling of my collar chimes. He picked me up again, exited the office, turned right and followed the passageway until it ended in a narrow rectangular room with a half dozen desks positioned along the two longer walls, three on each side. At the far end of the room a counter sectioned off a small area. My eyes were so filled with tears I was unable to distinguish anything beyond the counter. So this was it, my time was up and now I was going to disappear, without a trace, never to be heard from again. I didn't want to disappear, I wanted to go home, I wanted my parents. Suddenly I felt nauseated. A lump was swelling up in my throat, and I knew I was going to throw up. The man walked directly to the sectioned-off area, swung me up and sat me down on top of the counter, then asked, "Is this your cat?" It was a moment or two before reality sank in.

"Honeybee Ann Grant!" She always called me Honeybee Ann when she was upset with me. "Where have you been? I've been worried sick about you." An angel's voice couldn't have sounded sweeter. When she dragged me from the ugly plastic box and held me tight against her breast I knew I was not going to disappear. I was going home.

I don't remember much about what happened in the next few minutes. I was in a daze. My mother and I were both crying, but I vaguely recall my father paying a hefty fine plus the cost of my daily rations and the little green box. I also remember him getting a lecture on the "leash law" and saying "Yes sir," and "Thank you," several times. I was very sorry I

60

had caused my father so much trouble and my mother so much anguish; they could rest assured it would never happen again. My father took me from my mother's arms and stuffed me back inside the little box. I wasn't sure why, something to do with transporting pets in carriers, but it wasn't important. Nothing mattered except my parents were here and I was going home.

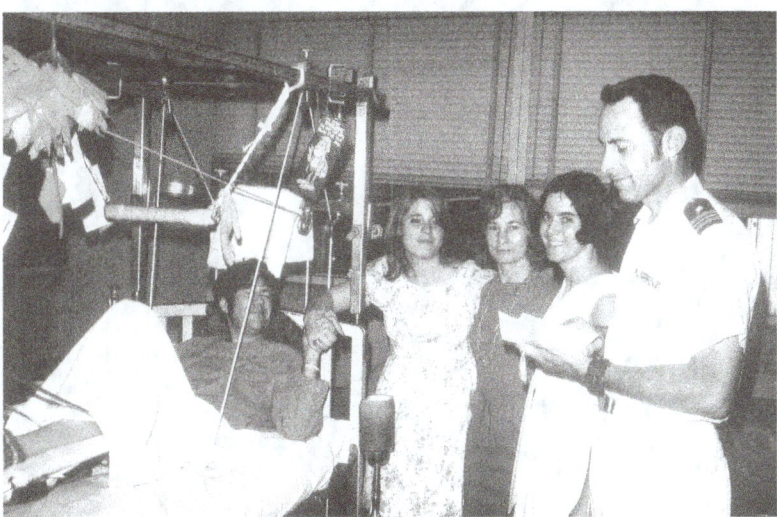

This took place before I was born. Nevertheless, it was how my family-to-be came to be. My mother, a "Doughnut Dolly" had just returned from her second tour of Viet Nam when she met my father at the Balboa Naval Hospital in San Diego. They married a few months later, thus setting the stage for my adoption and a life I would not have otherwise experienced. I was very fortunate.

61

62

Chapter V
A Day At The Beach

My father was up early the next morning; by the time my mother returned from her morning run he had the El Camino hooked up to the Airstream ready to go. An hour later we were driving along Mission Bay's perimeter road toward Interstate 5.

One would have thought on my first night home after being released from prison I would have slept like the proverbial kitten, but it didn't happen. I barely slept at all. Events of the last few days played across my subconsciousness, all twisted together in a psychedelic haze as I drifted in and out of a fitful sleep. It was always the same. I was locked in our old house in Bonita with all the inmates from the animal shelter. A man in an Animal Control uniform made trip after trip taking prisoners away until I was left all alone and then, upon hearing his footsteps and realizing he was coming for me, I would awake with a start, only to drift back into the nightmare that had awakened me in the first place.

63

As we took a southbound ramp onto Interstate 5 and headed into the city, I vacated my spot on the back of the front couch where I rode most of the time and moved to my old spot behind the other couch. The back of the couch was my favorite place to ride; today, however, I wasn't interested in the panoramas drifting past my window. City skylines can be impressive from a distance, but how can anyone prefer concrete sidewalks illuminated by streetlights to a moonlit meadow, or the roar of speeding traffic to the sigh of the wind in a forest, or exhaust fumes to the fragrance of night-blooming wildflowers?

I may have dropped off to sleep because I was unaware of how much time had passed or how far we had traveled, but I knew we were slowing down and instinctively extended my claws into the carpet to avoid being overcome by inertia. We continued to slow; seconds later we made a right turn and came to a stop.

It may have been that I just wanted to remember my last ride in the Airstream or perhaps it was emotion that elevated my perception. Be that as it may, I still remember everything that happened after we stopped as though it were yesterday. I heard the El Camino's doors slam shut, heard my parents approaching, heard the key slide into the lock, heard the bolt retract and felt the trailer sway as the door opened and they entered. I knew exactly what to expect, I listened as the water pump forced water through the system and out an open tap into a metal container, heard the zip of an electronic match and the accompanying whoosh as the propane burner ignited. A few minutes later the aroma of freshly brewed coffee reached my nostrils. The usual sounds followed, a spoon clinking against the side of a cup as my father stirred cream into his coffee, the crinkling of plastic wrap as my mother unwrapped bran muffins she had baked the night before.

"It sure is good to finally get out of San Diego," my mother remarked. What did she say? Did I hear correctly? What did she mean? I perked up my ears so as not to miss anything.

"It sure is, I thought we'd never get away. We could have left a couple of days earlier if the Big Dummy hadn't gotten herself thrown into the pound."

I heard my father shift positions and knew he was looking towards my hiding place when he exclaimed, "Get out here, you ugly little varmint. I know you're hiding back there." He waited a few seconds before speaking again.

"Well, I'd be ashamed to show my face, too, if I were you." He hesitated a moment or two, for effect I suppose, before adding, "Jailbird." I was to hear this nickname and suffer the embarrassment of its implications for some time to come.

Life on the road was good. The Southwest wasn't my cup of tea—there were few trees and hunting was the pits. However, there were some advantages. Most days were sunny and many areas, like the Painted Rock Mountains in Arizona, provided for a good dust bath and a snooze in the sun.

I slowly crawled out from behind the couch. Not because of my father's good-natured ribbing, but because of what my mother had said. As I emerged from my hidey-hole my parents were looking directly at me; embarrassed, I turned my head slightly to avoid eye contact.

"Well, I hope you're happy now that you've caused everybody so much trouble and worry?"

He was correct in one sense, I was happy, happy to be out

65

of jail, but very sorry for the anguish I had caused my parents. They could rest assured it would never happen again.

As I looked around I realized we were not in Bonita. We were at a rest stop and my parents were having coffee—when getting underway after an extended stay at any one place it had become traditional for my parents to stop at the first available rest stop, have coffee and check our rig for any telltale signs of trouble. A multitude of sensations surged through my entire being. All my stress and worries were swept away in a single stroke. We were on the road again! We were not going to live in Bonita, we were going to live in our trailer! We were Fulltimers! Suddenly I was starving.

My parents always sought out historical places as we traveled around the country, so for the first couple of months that winter we zigzagged across the Southwest climbing about the ruins of ancient cliff dwellers and walking the streets of old ghost towns where famous desperadoes had been gunned down by courageous and equally famous lawmen when justice was quick and precise. We searched out Indian strongholds, old forts, and battlegrounds, followed the trails of the great cattle drives, and marveled, as did the pioneers of a century past, at the Marfa Mystery Lights rolling across the desert floor.

The Southwest was okay, I guess. It was a lot better than living in the city, but once we crossed the Mississippi River I found myself in a world more to my liking. Hundreds of different sounds emanated from the swamps and bayous. Tasty little critters were everywhere. I loved it. I spent practically every waking moment outside. Swamps were no different than any other place, inasmuch as danger was always near at hand. Snakes were everywhere. They were on pathways, behind rocks, stumps, and decaying logs, as well as on trees and in the water. Most were harmless, but ever since my encounter with the rattler in Death Valley I've never liked snakes and always give them a wide berth.

Our first stop, east of the Mississippi, was Longfellow-Evangeline State Commemorative Area. After two months in the desert, this was the Garden of Eden. Gnarled undergrowth hid little green meadows; majestic cypress grew out of the swamps and marshes, and any pool of water, no matter how

66

small, contained delectable little lobsterlike critters I came to know as "craydads." My introduction to the craydad proved to be quite painful, but after I learned to avoid their powerful claws I found them to be delicious. My parents ate them by the dozens. It's safe to say, when we left Cajun Country there were far fewer crayfish than when we arrived.

Sometimes, it seemed to me, my parents would get really weird ideas, or perhaps they went out of their way, from time to time, just to bug me. On one such occasion, they decided to drive a couple of hundred miles just to take a swim in the ocean. Actually it was the Gulf of Mexico, but to me it was one and the same; if I can't see across it, it's an ocean.

Grand Isle State Park is a barren spit jutting out into the Gulf; nothing more than a small desert next to a lot of water, if you ask me. We paid our fee at the entrance station and were told to camp anyplace we liked. I remember some discussion about *sleeper waves* and it was suggested that we not park too close to the water. I didn't like anything about Grand Isle and was relieved when my father left the El Camino hooked up to the Airstream. Not disconnecting meant we wouldn't be staying long.

I was born in Coronado and spent my early kittenhood close enough to the Pacific Ocean to hear its voice. It was hypnotic and soothing when it murmured and whispered, but frightening when it boomed and roared. Sometimes, when it fell silent, I would forget all about it until I smelled the fresh breezes laden with salt, fish, and seaweed, or it sent a blanket of fog creeping across the street, obscuring everything from sight. However, strange as it may seem, the Pacific was still a mystery; I had never actually seen it. I was never permitted to cross Ocean Boulevard which separated our front yard from the beach. Now, I was finally going to see the ocean and although I should have been excited, uneasiness ruled my emotions. I had bad vibes about Grand Isle.

In no hurry to venture outside, I sat in the open doorway looking out across a narrow stretch of sand at nothing but water as far as the eye could see. So, this was the ocean. I was disappointed. I guess, since it had always been something mysterious and foreboding known to me only by smells and sounds, I had expected more.

67

My father had just finished gathering driftwood for our evening campfire when my mother asked if he would like to go for a walk. When he answered in the affirmative I decided it was time to see if I could find anything of interest and leapt outside as my mother approached the door. When they headed across the little desert toward the water I decided to tag along and sprinted after them. It was difficult to keep up. Each time my paw touched down it sank into the loose sand and when I tried to push off on the next step it would slip out from under me, resulting in a stumbling, sliding gait that required lots more energy than walking on grass or any other solid footing. I called out to them, hoping they would slow down and allow me to catch up. My mother's ears must have been tuned to my voice because she always heard me anytime I was within range. Seeing my plight, she came back, picked me up and hurried after my father. He waited for us and we walked the rest of the way to the ocean together. As we neared the water I squirmed a bit. It was my way of saying, "Put me down." My mother complied with my wishes and deposited me, to my surprise, on a hard damp surface. The sand near the water was packed hard, almost like a sidewalk.

I sat watching waves race up the little hill at the water's edge and listened to the strange gurgling sounds as they slid slowly back toward the sea. It was always the same, a wave would run up the beach, then fall back toward the ocean to be met by another surge of water coming ashore. My parents removed their shoes and began wading in the water, moving back and forth with the ebb and flow.

Losing another bout to curiosity—a battle I and my kind are doomed to fight until the end of time—I gave in to a sudden urge to taste a wave. I reasoned that if I timed my approach just right I should be able to taste the water without getting wet. I crept slowly down the little hill to meet the incoming wave. To my surprise, just as the wave turned it sank into the sand, leaving nothing but foam. I waited for the next wave to crest—the same thing happened. When the third wave came in I followed it down the beach to a point where a ridge of sand slowed the water's retreat, creating a tiny pool. Aware that the next wave was already on its way, I lapped quickly from the pool. It was super salty,

68

really yucky. As I turned to scamper back up the beach and avoid the next incoming wave I realized that my feet were wet and covered with sand—anything sticking to my paws really bugs me—so I stopped to shake off the wet sand. Each time I succeeded in cleaning one paw and tried another, the paw I had just cleaned would become covered in sand again the moment I put it down. With such preoccupation I forgot about the incoming wave until I heard it. When I looked up and saw the wall of water coming right down on top of me I instantly knew this was no ordinary wave. This was the legendary sleeper wave the ranger had warned us about. I froze, unable to move. Time stood still and events unfolded in slow motion. I saw my parents scrambling to avoid the wave, heard my mother scream out my name, heard my father yelling, "Run, you big dummy!"

I recovered my senses and heeding my father's warning bolted headlong up the beach heading straight for the Airstream. My feet were barely touching down when I hit the loose sand; I stumbled and fell, rolling head over heels, but recovered without losing a step. Knowing the wave was about to wash over me and I was going to drown I dared not chance a backward glance for fear of losing a single moment, and sprinted even faster, if that was possible. As I approached the trailer I remembered my mother had closed and locked the door and I began looking for a tree. There were none in sight. The El Camino was my only hope. I sprang to the hood in a single bound, and another leap put me atop the cab. I braced for the moment the wave would hit. I waited. And waited. Nothing happened. I looked toward the ocean and couldn't believe my eyes. A few puddles at the edge of the loose sand were the only evidence the wave had ever existed. In a matter of seconds they, too, disappeared, soaking into the thirsty sand. My parents were strolling toward the trailer as if nothing unusual had happened. They weren't even wet! How could that be? Puzzled, I climbed down from my perch and waited for the trailer door to be opened.

"Wow!" My father exclaimed, "I never knew you were that fast. I think I'll enter you in the hundred-yard dash at the next Olympics." My mother picked me up, rocked me back and forth saying, "Don't you ever do that again." And then added as she gave me a big kiss, "I'll bet you were scared." Scared! She would never know how much.

We left early the next morning, which was none too soon for me. During our travels we've camped on more beaches than I can remember, but one thing is for sure, I'll never forget my first walk on the beach or the first time I saw the ocean. Grand Isle is imprinted indelibly on my mind.

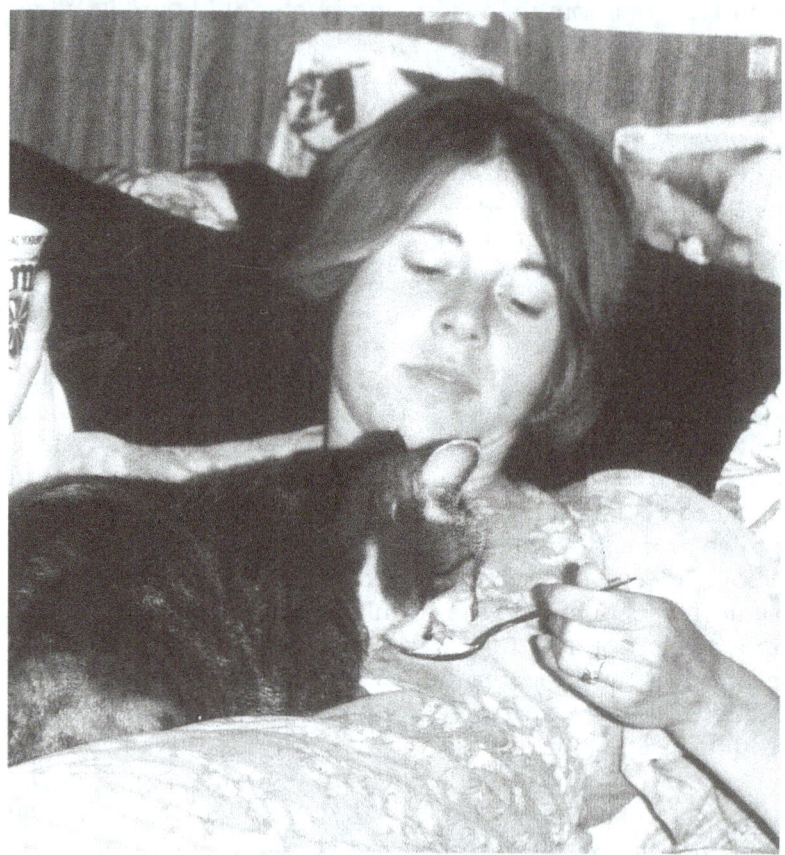

There were rainy days when we all just stayed inside and lounged about. I enjoyed these kick-back days when I could spend time with my parents. Rainy days also meant extra at-tention and extra treats.

70

Chapter VI
A Stroll In The Park

For the next couple of months, we worked our way along the Gulf of Mexico. From southeast Florida we cut across the Everglades, then followed the causeway through the Keys to its terminus at Key West, stopping whenever and wherever it suited us. I loved Fulltiming. There is no better feeling than, after tiring of one place, heading down the highway toward another new adventure. It may seem strange to some, but no matter how excited I might have been to arrive at a new place, it always looked better looking back. The one exception was Key West.

Ninety miles of bridges connecting dozens of islands, some nothing more than coral reefs, join Key West to the mainland. I wasn't all that excited about camping in the Keys since most camping is on the beach. A beach is nothing more than a stretch of desert with water on one side—the only water I get excited about is in a bowl beside my food dish. In the Keys there's water on both sides. You're surrounded by water, but

I was comforted just knowing we would soon move on to another place. When in Key West you're closer to Cuba than to the mainland—this tidbit I learned from Ernest. I learned a lot of things from Ernest. In a single night he stole my heart.

My parents spent three days visiting old friends and exploring Key West while I stayed locked in our trailer. On the last evening we were to spend in Key West our hosts decided to have a shrimp feast and I was allowed to come along. The shrimp were dipped right out of the canal from the floating

The Gulf Coast was okay, but the beach wasn't my thing. The water smelled funny, and the sand stuck to my feet and had a yucky taste when I licked it off. On the other hand, my parents loved the beach. They swam and walked along the sand while beachcombing, or my father fished in the surf or shot coins with his metal detector while my mother lay in the sun and read.

dock behind their house and thrown directly into a big pot of boiling water. After a few minutes in the big pot they were washed under running water and tossed into another pot filled with ice water. It all seemed a bit messy to me; however, they were quite tasty—my mother slipped me a couple under the table—but I wasn't all that hungry so while the others gorged themselves I wandered out onto the dock and was about to climb the gangway leading to our friends' boat when something caught my eye near the forward mooring lines. I turned, and there was Ernest. My heart rate doubled, I grew weak in the knees, and I thought I might even faint. I was in love.

72

We walked awhile without uttering a single word. Finally, after settling in the shadows, Ernest introduced himself and began to speak of his family. His great-great-great-grandfather, Ernest I, had been born in Havana and as a teenager wandered onto the boat of a certain writer-adventurer about to set sail for his home in Key West. During the ensuing trip the stowaway and the writer developed a friendship that would last a lifetime. According to Ernest VI, they were two of a kind. Both were popular with the ladies and as rumor had it,

My mother and I often took naps together. I had wonderful parents; it was good to be loved.

late-night rendezvous with secret lovers were not uncommon. I imagine most of those rumors were true and I suspect if one inquired after the reputation of Ernest VI, one would also find him popular with the ladies and similar rumors circulating about his nighttime social activities. Like great-great-great-grandfather, like great-great-great-grandson, I always say. At least Ernest VI was popular with this lady.

It was almost noon when I arrived home the next morning. My mother threatened to keep me locked up; my father asked if I had forgotten about the straitjacket. Still on cloud nine, I was oblivious to their ranting and raving. Leaving Key West was painful, but I knew it was for the best. I could never

73

have Ernest—he wasn't the type to be settled down by the likes of me. In the end he would surely have broken my heart. But I will always have my memories and, sometimes, when we are near the ocean and fresh salt air permeates the night I hide in the shadows and fantasize.

February had seen us move slowly up the Atlantic seaboard, campsite to campsite. With spring just around the corner, I knew it wouldn't be long before we began migrating north in search of a remote campground near a trout stream and best of all, far from the crowds. So I was surprised when my father pointed the El Camino inland heading almost due west. A light rain began falling shortly after we broke camp around five o'clock. Our early-morning departure told me this would be a long day. The rain was persistent and continued all morning and into the afternoon. Water thrown up by the El Camino created a muddy film on the Airstream's windows, making it difficult and sometimes impossible to see outside. Toward evening the rain stopped, the clouds began to disappear, and the sun shone briefly before slipping below the horizon. I was excited. We had left the main road and I knew we were nearing our destination.

It was well after dark before we arrived. I was waiting in my customary position by the door; when it opened I was outside and up a tree in a flash. As my eyes adjusted to the darkness, a fantasy world unfolded before me.

Huge cypress trees, crowned and bearded with Spanish moss, cast ghostlike shadows in front of a full moon that hung just above the horizon. Wisps of tulle fog crept through the trees, drifted in and out of the shadows and floated across the murky waters. The water, dark with tannin from thousands of ancient cypress trees, still and mirrorlike, cast back the ghostly scene before it. Mysterious voices intruded on the otherwise eerie silence as the swamp's inhabitants conversed in tongues only they understood. A peculiar odor, damp and earthy, permeated the night. This was my kind of place.

At least an hour passed, maybe even two or three—I often lose track of time—while I lay on a limb some twelve or fifteen feet above the ground, straining to glimpse evanescent movements in the shadows and listening to the sounds of the night. By the time the lights in the Airstream went out

74

most other campsites had already shut down. Only one campfire remained. A family of local bandits, complete with masks, padded silently toward the campfire, stopping only once to raid a nearby trash can. Just outside the ring of firelight they sat watching a couple roasting hot dogs, skewered onto long, skinny sticks, over the glowing embers. Their strategy, if indeed they were capable of advance planning, seemed simple enough, and worked beautifully. The two offspring advanced on the campers in a frontal attack while mother made a rear assault.

The youngsters went into their routine and began begging for food—their efforts were quickly rewarded with potato chips—while mother, avoiding detection, made her way to the picnic table. The youngsters continued their antics, to the delight of the campers, and received more potato chips for their efforts. In the meanwhile, mother, sticking to the shadows, climbed onto the picnic table and made off with the open package of hot dogs. Then, as suddenly as it had begun, as if by some prearranged signal, the performance was over and the young con artists joined their mother in the safety of the dense undergrowth along the water's edge, to feast on the stolen hot dogs.

The moon had climbed high into the night sky before hunger nudged my subconsciousness. From the comfort and safety of the tree limb I had familiarized myself with the lay of the land, committing everything to memory in preparation for the ensuing hunt, and it was now time to probe those intriguing shadows and seek out the individuals hiding in the dark whose mysterious voices reverberated in the night. Some would surely be tasty. Hunting was good and my appetite soon satiated. I groomed myself, rested a bit, and then set off to further explore this place called trembling earth—known to most as Okefenokee.

A short distance past the campground entrance the road ended in front of a long single-story building. I walked along a deck that ran the entire length of the building and upon reaching the opposite end continued down a ramp to where a few small boats, most not much bigger than our canoe, were tied to a rickety dock. Finding nothing of interest on the dock I decided to follow the narrow channel that led from

75

the small marina to what I suspected was the heart of the Okefenokee. Following the channel, I walked across a well-manicured lawn until it ended in what might best be described as a jungle. As I entered the jungle I realized I was also entering the swamp, where trees and thick undergrowth grew right up out of the water. I was about to head back toward the marina when I spotted a half-submerged log which served as a ready-made bridge over the water and provided a path through the trees. By leaping to a second log, then a third, and continuing from one to another, I found easy traveling on a trail that carried me ever deeper into the swamp.

I spotted a small hummock about four feet away and sprang almost effortlessly to its grassy surface and felt it quiver underneath my weight as I landed—thus the name, trembling earth. A bullfrog resting on the hummock croaked his resentment, at what he no doubt considered a rude encroachment on his otherwise peaceful retreat. He jumped from the hummock to a clump of lily pads some ten feet away. The hummock, perhaps six feet across, was indeed peaceful and seemed like a perfect place to rest and maybe take a short nap.

Unaware of how long I had slept, I awoke with a start and a genuine but unexplainable uneasiness. The fog had all but disappeared; however, visibility was now limited and illusionary. The moon, moving steadily toward the western horizon cast ever lengthening shadows that were ominous and foreboding, and hid only heaven knew what. When an occasional puffer belly drifted past the moon obscuring everything to all but the keenest eye, I found the swamp less enchanting. I struggled to maintain control of my imagination. Any unidentified sound or movement became frightening, and at times bordered on terrifying. Unsure of how deep into the swamp I had come and not being absolutely positive of the route I had taken did nothing to relieve my anxiety.

I was all set to leap onto a log where I believed the trail began that would carry me back to the marina when I noticed another cumulus cloud on a collision course with the moon. Filtered moonlight penetrated the fluffy cloud at first but faded rapidly as the puffer belly engulfed the moon completely and painted the landscape pitch-black.

76

As I waited in the darkness to exit the hummock a disturbing image registered in my subconsciousness. Before the cloud obliterated the moon, I had been watching an odd-shaped log floating towards the little grassy hummock and now realized the rate of its drift far exceeded the current—the Okefenokee is actually a river inching its way toward the Gulf of Mexico via the Suwannee—and in those last few seconds just before the moon disappeared I glimpsed what appeared to be eyes. I told myself I had only imagined it; logs do not have eyes. Although I continued trying to reassure myself, reasoning that the swamp's ominous overtones were playing tricks on my imagination, I realized my heart was racing. When I felt the little hummock tremble and heard a splashing sound, I panicked. I was about to leap blindly toward the trail when the moon finally broke free of the puffer belly and I was able to see again. The sight before me struck sheer terror through every fiber of my being. Not two feet away, in the middle of my intended path, was a mouth, three feet long, open at ninety degrees, with no less than a hundred teeth. I didn't need a second look—I reacted out of fear and instinct that unleashed power in my haunches I never knew existed and literally flew over the jaws of death onto the log path. The next thing I knew I was on the grass by the marina, not realizing how I had gotten there or how long it had taken me. My heart sounded as though it was about to burst out of my chest, I was gasping for air, and my legs were turning to jelly, but I continued to run and didn't stop running until I was in a tree overlooking the Airstream. As my heart rate came down and my breathing returned to normal I reflected on my close encounter and considered that just maybe, this wasn't my kind of place after all.

I remained close to the trailer for the rest of our stay, sleeping mostly. My parents loved the park; they explored on foot and in our canoe during the day, then at night, while sitting around the campfire feeding scraps to the raccoons, I would hear them discussing the many wonders of the swamp, including the number of alligators they had counted that day. Well, they could count all the alligators they wanted—one was more than enough for me.

Now and again I would hear, from different people, some reference to the supposition that members of my species have nine lives. Each time, upon hearing this mentioned, I wondered just how many lives I had left. I knew for sure, I had one less when we left the Okefenokee swamp than I had when we arrived.

Chapter VII
The Bog Wants You

For the rest of that winter and most of the spring my parents' passion for history took us on a meandering journey up the East Coast as we searched out our heritage. Our unhurried explorations took us from the birthplace of Virginia Dare on Roanoke Island to the birthplace of the American Revolution at Lexington, from Kill Devil Hills, where man first defied Earth's gravity to Cape Canaveral, where man had escaped earth's gravity. On and on we searched. Sometimes my parents seemed possessed by a quest for knowledge and their desire to live in the past and experience every event in our country's history. My mother kept a journal of our travels, making entries each night before going to sleep. I will never know for sure why she kept such meticulous records, but I always suspected her intent was to leave a written record of our own personal history.

I wasn't into history very much. I concerned myself mostly with the present while only occasionally pondering the fu-

79

ture or looking back at the past. My father believed understanding the past was the key to making sound decisions and planning for the future. Perhaps he was right. I knew experience had taught me to avoid many dangers. I would never again be lured into a trap or be caught by a sleeper wave and I would most certainly avoid alligators, coyotes,

As you can see, it was Christmastime in the city and I had my stocking hung, hoping for a visit from Saint Nicholas. Both my parents seemed to have a need to write things down; my mother spent a few minutes each day writing in her journal. During the summer my father sometimes wrote for an hour or two in a notebook, and then put it away for a week and sometimes a month or more before writing in it again. Once we moved out of Bambi and back into the Royals, he'd peck away on a noisy little typewriter transcribing what he had written in his notebook. I never knew what he wrote about.

and eagles. Still, I pretty much believed what had already happened couldn't be changed and what was to come would happen anyway. I considered my father very wise, but we made decisions by different formulas; logic guided him whereas emotion ruled my life. That is not to say my father was uncaring and without feeling, neither is it to say I always leaped before looking, but I found logic too complicated and time consuming while decisions based on pure emotion provided for spur-of-the-moment action. This might explain why I often found myself in unpleasant situations, and, no doubt, led to my father's tagging me with another nickname, "Troublesome Tabby." But, what the heck, I wasn't supposed to be able to reason or consider the outcome of my actions beforehand, which provided the basis of my philosophy; if it feels good, do it. This kind of thinking probably got me into my next bit of trouble which earned me a nickname even more embarrassing than Jailbird.

We spent the better part of May and June in New England. Life for me was pretty much back to normal. Although the wee hours of morning were still chilly, I stayed out most nights mousing and exploring, and spent the days sleeping and dreaming. Often my dreams were of another time and another place where I interacted with creatures unlike any I had ever seen; yet they were not unfamiliar. I didn't know the meaning of my dreams and I no longer tried to analyze them, in time I would surely understand.

My father was again doing what he seemed to enjoy most, fishing. He would leave early in the morning, wearing a funny-looking outfit he called waders and carrying his fly rod. A couple of hours later he'd return carrying a mess of trout. My mother hiked, took pictures, wrote letters, lounged in the sun, read, and, of course, kept her journal. Life was good.

Toward the end of June we crossed the Saint Lawrence Seaway into Canada. The only thing I noticed different was the way Canadians manage to turn a statement into a question, eh? It was a bit confusing at first, but in time became second nature, eh?

I recognized the signs—chilly nights, shorter days, a hint of color in the trees—and knew summer was nearing its end. It had passed too quickly. I wasn't surprised when a few days later we packed up and headed south. I wasn't worried; this didn't signify an end to our travels, as I had suspected and feared a year ago. It was only an indication we were heading to a warmer climate for the winter. We were *snowbirds*.

We traveled slowly, sometimes spending several days exploring an area we found interesting. By the time we reached the Finger Lakes in Western New York the leaves had taken on colors of such brilliance they caused the ones I had seen

81

the previous autumn, when I had seen red-and gold-colored leaves for the first time, to pale by comparison.

We stopped in the small town of Watkins Glen and bought groceries, purchased a part for the El Camino, had a propane bottle filled, and topped off the gas tank. I was able to observe everything while comfortably sprawled on the back of

One of the great things about RV-ing is the ability to change the scenery outside your window by turning the ignition key and relocating your house in as little time as a day or even an hour. When the weather changes or you desire a change of scene you can move on to a new and exciting place or revisit an area you enjoyed before. In autumn New England is a fairyland with leaves of red and gold shimmering in the sun and floating on the breeze like tiny sailboats with colored sails. The nights are cool, the air is sweet, and there are plenty of little critters to harass and lots of trees to climb.

the front couch—my normal travel station. At our fourth stop my parents spent a long time inside a building with black and white checkered flags flying from a dozen different positions. Above the door a large banner proclaimed the building to be "Grand Prix Racing Association Headquarters."

In the early afternoon we set up camp in a wooded area a few miles outside town and when the door finally opened I was, as usual, outside and up a tree in a flash. The sun through the trees set the leaves ablaze with such radiance that, with-

82

out knowing, one might presume them to be self-illuminating; it was a fairyland.

There are many advantages in climbing trees. Climbing a tree enables one to escape one's enemies, to relax comfortably while remaining safe from prying eyes and whatever dangers might be lurking below, and to see great distances and survey the surroundings from afar. I looked long and hard in all directions without spotting another camper. Apparently we were all alone, which suited me just fine. A few feet in front of our trailer the dirt road we had followed to our campsite continued and disappeared in the trees. Across the dirt road and perhaps two hundred feet away were several small buildings, without doors or windows, all strung out in a row. On either side of the buildings were huge scaffold-like structures. I couldn't imagine their purpose, neither could I think of a use for a building without windows or doors. Oh well, I would check all this out tonight, maybe then I would be able to figure out their purpose since for the moment the warm sunshine was making me drowsy, and with a nice comfortable tree limb underneath me I couldn't resist closing my eyes and letting nature take its course. I was dreaming almost immediately.

I was awakened by an unfamiliar voice asking questions of my parents. Curious as to what was going on, I climbed down and walked over to where my parents and the stranger were relaxing in canvas folding chairs that matched perfectly the Airstream's blue and white awning. The stranger was surprised when I leapt onto my mother's lap, with my I-want-to-know-what's-going-on-here greeting, and directed his attention and next couple of questions at me. I, of course never talked to strangers and made no exception of him, letting my parents answer for me, as I knew they would. After a few more questions and some idle conversation, the stranger took our pictures and prepared to leave; it was then I realized, when he picked up his cassette recorder, our conversations had been taped. I was a bit curious about the tape recorder, but by now I was getting bored with the whole thing and my thoughts shifted to food. I headed for the trailer and my Purina Stars.

It was already dark when I awoke. I was anxious to get

83

outside, but decided first to stop by my food dish for a quick snack. I had learned early on in my travels that the availability of food varied from place to place. It would be foolish of me to assume food would be plentiful in these new and unfamiliar surroundings. My mother opened the door after my first call—by now I had her pretty well trained. Once outside the Airstream and after a leisurely stretch, a kind of Tai Chi routine, which I executed automatically without thinking—obviously something programmed by nature into my subconsciousness—I strolled to the middle of the dirt road and sat down. A harvest moon painted everything in sight and sent little fingers of light through the trees to probe the forest floor, lighting pathways for any woodland creature who might be out and about on this late September evening. I sat for some time watching the leaves, set free by the gently swirling breeze, drift like tiny sailing ships across the face of the moon and all the while wondering why I so loved the nighttime. It was a perfect night to explore, to seek out and unravel the mysteries behind the soft, scurrying sounds heard in the distance. Barely able to contain my excitement, I set out to discover the secrets of my new domain. First on my agenda were the strange buildings and the huge scaffolding-like structures, standing stark and silent in the moonlight.

Although excited, I took my time—it wasn't my nature to hurry. When I reached the row of buildings I found them all pretty much the same, about eight feet deep and anywhere from ten to fifteen feet long. They all had doors on one end, and attached to the side opposite our trailer were shelves that ran the entire length of each building. I walked around and underneath a couple of the buildings—they were built on skids and without permanent foundations—but found no way to get inside or even see inside. I made one last attempt to gain entry by leaping onto one of the shelves but, alas, it was to no avail.

I sat for a few moments thinking and listening to the night sounds before realizing a chain link fence stood only a few feet away from the row of buildings. A well-maintained highway ran parallel to and on the other side of the fence. To my right the highway disappeared over a low hill; off to my left it dropped out of sight around a long sweeping downhill curve. Across the highway and beyond another fence more scaffolding and several large buildings were visible in the moonlight.

I sat for several minutes pondering everything I had observed: a paved road without traffic, empty buildings without windows, scaffolding of steel and wood resembling something constructed from a giant erector set, and chain link fence everywhere. What did it all mean? Well, I wasn't going to figure out anything sitting on this shelf. With no particular plan in mind, I leapt to the ground and began walking along the fence toward the crest of the hill. A half hour later I reached the top of the hill. It wasn't much of a hill, more like a knoll. I chose a sugar maple with a nice fat limb about ten feet off the ground; a few seconds later I was resting comfortably in the maple tree.

There wasn't much to see. The fence and highway continued for another two or three hundred yards before, still running parallel to one another, they disappeared into the woods around a sharp high-banked curve. A narrow dirt road crossed underneath the highway through a short tunnel, but a locked gate prevented anyone from using the underpass. I was beginning to lose interest in these man-made mysteries; nature was my bag and it called to me from all directions. As I sat listening and watching, I became drowsy and dreams mingled with and became indistinguishable from reality. I interacted with creatures not unlike myself but with more massive bodies, shorter legs and tails, and long curved canine teeth. These creatures were not unfamiliar. I had met them before in my dreams.

By the time I awoke the moon had already passed its apex and was starting its descent toward the western horizon. The night air had cooled considerably, but this was to be expected. With the shorter days and longer nights and without cloud cover the earth would give up the heat it had collected from the sun's rays more rapidly than during the long days of summer. Actually, I preferred the lower temperatures and found the night air refreshing. It was good hunting weather and hunting was just what I had in mind. I was always hungry after a good nap and the fact that I hadn't eaten for almost three hours added an extra incentive—it was mousing time!

85

I loved climbing trees. With my sharp nails and powerful haunches I could literally fly up the trunk of a tree; however, getting down was a most embarrassing ordeal since it required backing down the tree trunk, slowly and carefully, until I felt safe enough to drop the rest of the way to the ground and landing, more often than not, in a disoriented heap. I always envied squirrels their ability to run headfirst up, down, and around a tree without ever losing their balance. With a good deal of scraping noise and the resulting thump, when I let go with my nails, I reached the ground, untangled myself, and headed for the woods behind our trailer. I couldn't see the Airstream now but from my position in the tree, with the moonlight reflecting off its aluminum body, it had been easy to spot and I now had a mental picture, not only of the Airstream's location, but of its relation to everything I had seen thus far.

My plan had been to cut across a large grassy meadow, avoiding the small muddy-looking area in the middle, until I reached the woods at a point about a hundred and fifty yards from our trailer, and then meander through the trees until I reached the Airstream. I would, no doubt, turn up a couple of fat mice along the way. I was surprised when, about a quarter of the way across the meadow, I found another fence blocking my path. Someone had fenced off the muddy area from the rest of the meadow. In order to reach the woods I had no choice but to walk along beside the fence until I reached a corner. Upon reaching the corner I turned toward the woods and continued walking alongside the fence. I had almost reached the next corner before I realized there were no gates. Someone had fenced off three or four acres, smack in the middle of the meadow, but had failed to install gates. There was absolutely nothing inside the fence except a few mud puddles. Protecting the mud puddles didn't seem logical. So who put up the fence and why? As I thought about the fence without gates and buildings without windows, I recalled other things that struck me as odd: there were no picnic tables, no fire rings nor, for that matter, any designated camping spaces. We had camped in some out-of-the-way places, but never anything this peculiar. Oh well, it wasn't any of my concern

86

and I wasn't about to waste my time trying to figure out all this weirdness.

Shortly after I entered the woods a barely audible sound stopped me in my tracks. I stared long and hard in the direction of the disturbance, but my eyes had not yet adjusted from the bright moonlit meadow to the dim shadows cast by the tree-filtered moonlight and I was unable to locate its source. I sat down and continued staring in the direction of the sound and as my night vision began to improve I finally detected a slight movement near a half-rotted stump. Cautiously and silently I made my way toward the stump until I was within pouncing distance. Just as I had suspected, a family of mice were living underneath the stump. I watched as they raced about gathering seeds, unaware death was lurking nearby. I was all set to pounce. Which one to eat first was the only thing on my mind, when I thought I heard someone or something digging or scratching on the far side of the stump. I listened intently. It came again or so I thought, but I couldn't be sure. With the leaves swirling and drifting about on the night wind it was difficult to determine if I had indeed heard something or perhaps, after all the weird things I had encountered tonight, I was just a bit jumpy. In an unfamiliar place it is sometimes easy for one's imagination to play tricks on the mind. The mice hadn't heard anything or if they had they didn't appear to be fearful or uneasy in any way. Hey, if they weren't worried, why should I be concerned? I put aside my misgivings, made my choice and sprang toward my intended midnight snack. I was in midair and unable to change my trajectory when I realized there was a drop-off immediately behind the stump. The stump sat on a ridge that ascended slowly from my side, but dropped off abruptly on the other side and from my previous position I had been unable to detect the drop-off. The mice had been playing along the top of the ridge and the one I had chosen was sitting on the very edge of the drop-off. Too late, I realized my mistake; needless to say, the mouse family would all live to enjoy another sunrise. I could have grabbed the mouse between my forepaws, but having become aware of my peril I lost all interest in my midnight snack. The bank's edge, unable to support my fourteen pounds, gave way underneath me and

87

my momentum sent me tumbling down the bank. I landed at the bottom covered with dirt and gravel loosened by my fall. I knew the moment I went over the edge I was in big trouble, but not from the fall.

She had been digging underneath the far side of the stump for grubs and termites when without warning I landed right beside her. Startled, she lost her footing and tumbled alongside me all the way to the bottom. In the dark I could only see her two white stripes, but that was enough, I knew the white stripes belonged to an otherwise jet-black skunk. The spray hit me even before I could disentangle myself from the dirt and gravel. It caught me full in the face; my eyes snapped shut and I could hardly breathe as a wave of nausea swept over me. I rubbed my face in the dirt, trying to rid myself of the foul-smelling liquid, but the stench had soaked into my fur and I couldn't get it out no matter how hard I tried. It seemed an eternity before the dry heaves stopped and the sickness began to subside. My breathing returned to normal and I was finally able to open my eyes enough to see. I stumbled back to the meadow and followed the tree line back to the Airstream. As I neared the trailer the door opened and my mother looked out. It was only then that I realized I had been howling my head off. She probably thought I was dying—from the way I felt she wouldn't have been far wrong. I had yet to fully recover and was still staggering, but afraid she might close the door, I steadied myself, put on an extra burst of speed and passed through the door just about the time my mother grabbed her nose.

I was starving. I had gone almost eight hours without eating but at the moment all I wanted to do was get in my hidey-hole and sleep. That, however, was not to be. My mother switched on a lamp, grabbed me by the nape of the neck, then clamped her free hand back over her nose. My father stirred only slightly at first, squinting against the light, then sat up as if zapped by lighting. He looked at my mother, still holding her nose with one hand and me at arm's length in the other hand, and began to laugh. I didn't find anything about my predicament amusing. My father looked down at me and shook his head, saying, as he cranked open a window, "You've got to be the dumbest cat that ever lived."

88

The next couple of hours saw me through an ordeal I don't wish to repeat, ever again. After opening all the windows and overhead vents, my father rummaged through the back of the El Camino until he found a five-gallon plastic bucket. We all moved to the bathtub where my mother, still holding me by the back of the neck, stuck me inside the bucket and held me down while my father opened the only two cans of tomato juice he could find and poured the sticky red liquid all over my body. He rubbed the tomato juice into my fur, stopping every so often to mumble some unflattering remark about my intelligence. I don't know if my father thought there wasn't enough juice or what, but for some reason, he opened a can of stewed tomatoes and dumped them on me, and to make matters worse, if that was possible, he took a bottle of tomato ketchup out of the refrigerator and added that to the mix. He continued to rub the liquid into my fur, which soaked up just about everything except the stewed tomatoes.

I was miserable, my eyes were stinging, my fur was a sticky mess, I was cold, tired, hungry and still smelled to high heaven. Just when I thought it couldn't possibly get any worse, out came the straitjacket; it would have been a waste of time and effort to resist. I had forgotten about the humiliating harness I was forced to wear after my Death Valley episode and as-sumed they had thrown the stupid contraption away. But here I was all strapped in and tied, with a very short leash, to the faucet in the bathtub.

I had been tied up in the bathtub for almost an hour when I heard approaching footsteps; the door slid open, the lights came on, and when I looked up I saw both my parents star-ing down at me. I must have been a pitiful sight. With the windows open and my fur soaked all the way through to my skin I was cold and starting to shiver. I must have looked like the proverbial drowned rat. When my mother looked at me she became very sad and for a moment I thought she was going to cry. My father knelt down, placed the stopper in the drain, and turned on the hot water.

"How did you get yourself into this mess?" he asked.

"If I'd known you were going to be so much trouble, I'd have named you Troublesome instead of Honeybee, yeah, Troublesome Tabby, that would be a good name for you."

89

He kept up a monologue of what I'm sure he thought were humorous remarks about the way I smelled. The water felt cold at first, then started to get warm. It felt good.

I detested a bath more than just about anything except this stupid straitjacket, but I wasn't going to complain if it got rid of the sticky tomato juice and the skunk odor. I wasn't sure which, but it seemed to me either the tomato concoction had worked or I was just getting used to the stink. Perhaps it was a little of both. I preferred to think it had worked. After getting rinsed several times my father started up our little generator and my mother used her hair dryer to dry and fluff my fur. I was beginning to feel much better and when she finished I headed towards the bathroom to locate my food dish, but to my surprise, my father picked me up, carried me outside, pointed out my food and water dishes, which were now under the trailer, then went back inside and closed the door.

By the time I finished eating, there was a faint glow spreading across the eastern sky. Dawn was breaking. Although I felt pretty good, considering all the things I had gone through, I was dead tired so I crawled up on one of the Airstream's tires and went to sleep.

It was midday when I was awakened by the sound of eighteen-wheelers. I crawled down off the tire, stretched, crunched a few Purina Stars, then climbed the tree behind the Airstream to see if I could figure out what was happening. Two trucks had passed through the tunnel and come to a stop in front of the largest building near the center of the compound. Fifty people, maybe more, were involved in various activities. Some stood around in little groups talking and pointing, others operated television cameras, while most of the people unloaded the big trucks. They unloaded about three dozen little cars off the trucks and pushed them into the large building. The shiny little cars were painted all sorts of colors and were pretty, but seemed impractical. They had what appeared to be wings in the rear, all were without fenders or tops, and had barely enough room for one person to fit inside, but, even more impractical was the ground clearance; they were only an inch or two off the ground and would surely drag the bottom on every bump in the road.

All this activity only served to raise more questions. Oh

well, I had problems enough without concerning myself with the goings on in the little village. I needed to figure out a way to move back inside the house. Roaming around at night and taking an occasional nap in a tree was one thing, but when it came to serious daytime sleeping there was no better place than my hidey-hole with my food and water dishes nearby. But for the time being, I was stuck with sharing my food and water with bugs and ants while using a trailer tire for a bed. The only comforting thought, if there was any consolation to be found in all of this—was that they hadn't insisted on me wearing the straitjacket. I sat by the door and complained, but all it got me was sympathetic conversation from my mother and a couple of not so sympathetic remarks from my father. After about half an hour, I gave up and climbed back onto the trailer tire and went to sleep.

It was well after dark when I awoke and crawled out from under the Airstream and was almost blinded by the bright lights that lit up the little village. I wasn't in the mood to go exploring, so I stayed close to home, hunting in the woods behind the trailer. Daybreak found me waiting outside the trailer door. I knew my mother would be doing her exercises, a prelude to her morning run and I was hoping to con her into letting me back inside the house. Again, all I got were sympathetic looks and phrases. Obviously, I was the only one getting used to skunk odor. Well, time for a nap. I ate a few crunches, lapped up some water, avoiding as many bugs and ants as I could, and climbed back up on the tire.

I had barely gotten to sleep or so it seemed, when I was awakened by an unfamiliar high-pitched revving sound which was coming from the direction of the little village. I dragged myself down off the tire and up the tree to see what was going on.

The little cars were speeding down the fenced-off highway; they kept coming by, one and sometimes two or three at a time, all going in the same direction. After a while I realized more cars passed than were unloaded. I was quite confused until I realized the highway ran in some sort of circle, similar to the racetracks mice build. Then it hit me. The little highway was a racetrack and the funny-looking cars were race cars. Well, at least one mystery was solved.

91

Next morning I awoke to the sound of the race cars whizzing by. They were annoying enough, but now all sorts of other noise was coming from the direction of the little village. Following the path I had worn in the grass between the trailer tire and the tree I climbed up to my lookout station.

People were everywhere, opening up the little buildings. There was all sorts of hammering and sawing as tables, benches and platforms were being built, some with awnings and big umbrellas. Several open-air tents had been erected. All sorts of stuff was being unloaded from cars, trucks, vans, and various other type vehicles. Some of the stuff went into the little buildings and some was stacked on the newly constructed tables. Also, campers had started showing up and were setting up camp, apparently, wherever they pleased. This was the most unorganized campground I had ever seen and no one seemed to care. It crossed my mind, and I can't explain why, but I had the distinct impression this was just the beginning. The thought was a bit disturbing, and yet, at the same time a tinge of excitement crept through my consciousness.

Later that day the guy with the camera and tape recorder stopped by. He was talking with my parents when I walked up and I guess my perfume was still a bit loud because he turned and looked at me and while trying not to laugh, he said, "I see you've met one of our local kitties." He must have thought I was stupid and most likely figured me for a city dweller who wouldn't know skunks were also known as polecats. This thing with the skunk was not only a problem—it was getting to be downright embarrassing. I just walked away.

My parents were standing together by the trailer door, reading a newspaper given them by the camera guy, when I walked over and jumped up on the step.

"Want to see your picture?" my mother asked, as she leaned over and held the paper in front of my face. Sure enough, there I was sitting in my mother's lap. It was a nice family picture with all of us in front of the Airstream underneath the pretty blue and white awning. I gave her my best, well-isn't-that-nice routine, hoping she would open the door and I could dash inside. She reached for the door handle and just

92

when I thought I was going to get lucky, my father reached down, picked me up, and holding me at arm's length, stuck me under the trailer. I crawled back up on the tire and fell asleep wondering when my quarantine would end, and how much longer before I would be allowed back inside the house.

Campfires glowed late into the night while over at the little village lights blazed so brightly it might as well have been daytime. I stayed close to home and for a second night did my hunting in the woods behind our trailer. Hunting was good, but my heart just wasn't in it. I just couldn't generate any enthusiasm, so I dragged myself up on my tire at a relatively early hour. I hadn't been myself since my encounter with the polecat and, with all the noise during the day, I hadn't been getting my beauty sleep and was beginning to feel a tad under the weather. Instinct told me tomorrow would be even noisier. I was right.

I had gotten used to the cars racing past and was still asleep when the first blast from the public address system made me jump, causing me to bump my head against the underside of the Airstream. I climbed down off my tire, stretched, ate a few Purina Stars along with several ants—they were crawling all over my food and couldn't be avoided. My water dish was covered with a dust film blown over from the road. I lapped up the dust with the water and headed for my tree. I knew it was my own fault for having to live this way and I understood my parents' position, but I sure would be happy when they let me move back inside where I would have ant-free food, dust-free water and a soft bed.

As dusk fell, campfires once again lit up the woods, glowing from horizon to horizon. There were ten or twenty and perhaps even fifty times as many as before and people were still coming. Hundreds of campers had arrived during the day and they were now arriving in even greater numbers. Dozens of tents were set up in the woods all around us. Two guys and a girl had erected a tent larger than our trailer, right underneath my tree. I wondered why they needed such a big tent. It could have easily slept twenty people. They busied themselves arranging things in the tent, gathering firewood, and cooking dinner on a propane camp stove by the light of a Coleman lantern. Whatever they were cooking smelled pretty

93

good. I wouldn't have minded having a sample and wondered if I put on my look-how-cute-I-am-face and strolled into their tent if they'd give me some. I decided it would be safer to wait until they were asleep—then I'd sneak down and see if there were any scraps left lying around.

A couple of hours later it appeared they were finally getting ready to go to bed. One of the guys turned the lantern down until it barely gave off any light at all; the girl brought a radio in from their van and turned it to a rock station. In the meantime, the other guy lit up a pipe, took a couple of drags and passed it to the second guy who took a couple of puffs before passing it to the girl. The smoke drifted up to where I lay sprawled on my limb and to my surprise it didn't smell like tobacco smoke. It was kind of sweet and spicy. I found it sickening. Of course, I didn't like tobacco smoke of any kind. They kept passing the pipe around to one another; every so often someone would refill it and start the whole thing all over again. The smoke kept drifting up to where I lay sprawled on my limb; there was a smoke fog throughout the tree. I was beginning to think it would go on all night and was about to give up waiting and go to sleep, when at long last they extinguished the lantern, turned off the radio, and crawled into their sleeping bags.

I had almost fallen asleep myself when I heard snoring coming from inside the tent and decided it was time to see if they'd left any goodies lying around. When I stood up and stretched I felt a little dizzy and light on my feet. I felt so light on my feet I was barely touching the limb; it was as though I was floating. For a moment or two I considered, rather than wasting time climbing down the tree, simply jumping to the ground. I felt as though I could glide, just like a bird, right down to the ground. Fortunately, I changed my mind and started walking along the limb toward the tree trunk. As I neared the trunk, I decided to climb down head first, like a squirrel, but before climbing down I would run around the trunk a couple of times. To make a long story short, on the way to the ground I bounced off a couple of lower branches, landed on the awning, which acted like a trampoline and threw me into a bush underneath the tree. I got up slowly and discovered, to my surprise, I hadn't broken any bones.

94

Even more surprising was the fact that I didn't feel any pain; actually, I didn't feel anything at all. Something told me I should stay home, so I elected to put off looking inside the big tent until later and headed for my tire.

The next morning I awoke to the same sounds, racing cars and blaring loudspeakers. When I dragged myself off the tire I was sore and stiff. I winced with pain as I attempted my morning stretch. Walking was just as bad. I wasn't sure I could make it up the tree, so with a couple of leaps that made my muscles feel like they were on fire, I climbed to the top of the El Camino.

Activity had really picked up from the day before. It was still early in the day, but new campers were arriving in a steady stream. There must have been thousands or tens of thousands, maybe even a hundred thousand—I had no way of knowing. I had never seen so many people in one place before. They arrived in cars, campers, vans, old buses, and on motorcycles. Some were walking and carrying backpacks. People were everywhere; they wandered back and forth, drove up and down the road in front of our trailer, climbed and sat on the scaffolding, and all the while more and more were arriving. It was crazy. However, another mystery had unraveled itself. The sections of wall, above the shelves that ran along one side of the little windowless houses were now completely open and folks were lining up outside to buy all sorts of sandwiches served on paper plates and drinks in big paper cups, as well as articles of clothing, camping supplies, posters, magazines, and a whole host of other things.

Late that afternoon four more people arrived and stowed their sleeping bags and other personal stuff inside the big tent behind our trailer. By dark a total of fifteen had moved into the tent and a noisy party was in full swing. I didn't want to take a chance climbing the tree tonight, I wasn't even sure I could, so I decided to check out the woods. Tents were in every little clearing; their campfires lit up the night and cast flickering shadows through the trees. Several campers had turned in early. Many had left their garbage, with some pretty tasty leftovers, outside their tents. Although I preferred eating my food out of a clean dish, there were a few advantages to dumpster dining. By the time I found my way back to the

Airstream the party in the big tent was winding down, and some, obviously already partied out, had crawled into their sleeping bags. As the others were preparing to do the same, someone asked in a loud whisper, "Anybody want to go to the Bog?"

"Yeah, let's go!" came a quick reply with an obvious rush of excitement. The excitement spread instantly through those not yet in bed and in what seemed like no time at all, five guys and three girls were on their way to the Bog, whatever and wherever that might be. For some unexplainable reason, I wasn't surprised when they headed toward the fenced-off meadow.

Earlier in the evening I had wondered about the cheering coming from the direction of the meadow and had considered investigating, but I hadn't recovered from falling out of the tree and even curiosity couldn't overcome stiff joints and sore muscles. Still, I was intrigued; at times it reminded me of the yelling and cheering at a football game during a touch-down and at other times there wasn't much noise at all. These cycles continued even at this late hour—loud at times, then dying away until I would forget all about it. Maybe tomorrow night I would investigate the meadow, but tonight I would stay close to home and when everyone was sleeping I'd check out the big tent.

No one inside the big tent had moved in over an hour. Other than a radio, a chorus of snoring was the only sound to be heard. The walls of the big tent were staked down all the way around, but unlike the tent my parents used for back-packing, the big tent had no floor, so it was easy to get inside by crawling underneath the wall between the stakes.

I waited a few minutes until my eyes adjusted to the dark-ness. Things had sure changed. The initial threesome had laid everything out neat and orderly with cots set up along each wall. Now stuff was thrown everywhere, eating and cooking utensils were still dirty, some half filled with uneaten food. Dozens of smelly bottles were scattered around and piled in the corners. Several paper cups containing liquid with the same pungent aroma as the bottles, some almost full, sat underneath the cots. I took a few bites from a nearby plate which, although a bit too salty for me, tasted pretty

96

good. I looked around for some water to quench my thirst, brought on by the salt, but the only liquid to be found was the odd-smelling stuff in the paper cups. I didn't want to waste time by making a trip to my water dish under the trailer— there were too many goodies lying around—but I did need something to rid my mouth of the salt. What the heck, I had tasted my father's tea when he wasn't looking and it wasn't all that bad. I'd give the stuff in the paper cup a try. When I lapped at the liquid it foamed up and tickled my nose. It tasted kind of bitter, but was otherwise okay. I must have been quite thirsty—before I realized it, I had drunk all the liquid in the cup. I took a couple more bites of the salty food, then started looking for another cup. Oddly, by the time I emptied the second cup my stiffness began to disappear and after a little more food and another cup of the strange-smelling liquid, which was beginning to taste pretty good, the soreness in my muscles had all but disappeared. I was feeling pretty good. I emptied three more cups before I decided to go home and by that time all my pain was gone and I was feeling real good. But something wasn't quite right, although I couldn't figure out what. It took three tries before I was able to crawl under the tent wall. Once outside, I had trouble walking; my back legs tried to pass my front legs a couple of times and my vision was kind of blurry. I breathed in the cold fresh air and for a moment or two everything seemed okay. During those few moments I saw the tree and decided to climb up to my old lookout station. I made a dash for the tree and while on the dead run I sprang towards the trunk, but something unexplainable happened. My front legs collapsed at the exact instant the muscles in my rear legs uncoiled; what was supposed to be a giant leap that would take me six feet up the side of the tree sent me tumbling and crashing into the tree trunk. Unable to get up at first, I tried to figure out what had happened and when I did finally get my feet under me and attempted to take a step, I fell down again. I looked over at the tree. There were now two trees. I blinked and shook my head, then looked again. No there was just one, but before I could look away, the one tree became two again. What was happening to me? I was getting scared. I looked in the direction of the trailer and saw two Airstreams.

97

Now I was really scared. I started howling as loud as I could as I stumbled toward the first of the two trailers.

Finally my mother opened the door and looked out. She watched me for a few seconds and went back inside to wake my father. His first words were, "What's she done now?" He turned on the floodlight above the door and stepped outside while my mother stood in the doorway. I could see them, but not clearly; they faded in and out of focus and at times everything went black and I couldn't see them at all. What was happening to me? Was I going blind? I was no longer just plain scared, I was in a panic. I was still stumbling toward the trailer door when my mother asked a question, in a hushed voice that sent sheer terror through every fiber of my being. "Do you think the skunk might have been rabid?"

"It's possible," my father answered in a whisper. "Skunks are known to carry rabies." He approached in a slight crouch and peered down at me.

"She does appear to have some froth around her mouth, but I can't really tell."

My heart stopped. I had rabies. I was going to die. My father had moved closer and while still staring down at me, asked my mother to bring him a towel. She disappeared from the doorway and reappeared a few seconds later with a heavy bath towel. Holding the towel out in front of him, like a shield, my father approached once again. He knelt down and threw the big towel over the top of me and quickly rolled the towel up with me inside. I knew I wasn't capable of resisting and didn't try. Actually, I didn't want to resist because his touch, even through the towel, was comforting. He carried me closer to the light, then slowly and carefully exposed my face. When I looked up and saw the anguish expressed in his face all hope deserted me. I had rabies. I would go mad and then die—it was only a matter of time. My father held me up close to the light and after a moment or two his expression became more puzzled than troubled. He moved his face very close to mine and sniffed a couple of times. A wide grin spread across his face and he began to laugh. Still laughing he looked over at my mother and said, "She's not rabid, she's drunk." He put his face close to mine again and looking directly into my eyes said, "You little sot."

98

Everything began to turn black again and I knew I was about to pass out. I didn't know what to expect, but I could tell from my father's laugh that being drunk was a lot better than being rabid.

I squinted at the bright sun shining through the window and was elated to find myself back in the house. I tried moving and found that all my old pains had returned with a vengeance along with several I didn't have before running into the tree. My head felt like it would explode, all my joints and muscles were stiff, and the slightest movement sent pain shooting through every inch of my body. Even my fur hurt. I had experienced my first and last "drunk" and vowed never to get into trouble again, but for now, all I wanted was for the pain to go away.

I slept soundly, except for the unusual number of trips to the sandbox, until early evening. I got up and slowly stretched my legs. My joints were only slightly stiff, my muscles no longer burned when I moved, and my head had stopped hurting, except when I crunched my Purina Stars or lapped water. I felt pretty good. All I needed was some fresh air and I would be good as new.

When I sauntered up to the door and uttered my I-want-to-go-outside request, my parents looked at each other for several seconds without speaking. Eventually, my mother queried, "What do you think?" When I repeated my request I turned up the volume. My father looked over at me and I pleaded to him in an even louder voice. He then asked, "Do you want to listen to her howl all night?" Without answering, my mother got up and opened the door.

I passed up the tree behind the Airstream and climbed up onto the El Camino instead. I felt okay, but decided to stay clear of the tree. It was responsible, in one way or another, for all my aches and pains and besides, the crazy smoke was drifting out of the big tent again. Well, something made me do crazy things and I will always believe it was the funny smoke.

People were everywhere; they all seemed to be going someplace or coming from someplace. Nobody seemed content with where they were at any one time. The cheering and yelling coming from the direction of the meadow was even

99

louder than before. Questions kept going through my mind. Why did crowds gather there every night? What were they cheering about? Why did they get so excited? When people passed one another on the road in front of the trailer they would ask questions like, "Have you been to the Bog?" "Are you going to the Bog?" "What's happening at the Bog?" Curiosity finally got the best of me; I stood up, stretched, and climbed down off the El Camino. How could I possibly get into trouble if I stayed well clear of the crowd? I would be very careful and work my way through the edge of the woods and when I was close enough to see the bog I would climb a tree, it surely wouldn't hurt anything to just take a peek.

An hour later I selected a large maple at the wood's edge and quickly climbed to one of the upper branches. I had chosen well—I had a great view.

I couldn't believe my eyes. The chain link fence that had surrounded part of the meadow had been flattened, posts and all. In the area once encircled by the fence, several fires were sending flames and heavy black smoke high into the night sky. At first I wasn't aware of what fueled the fires, but when a large group pushed a car across the flattened fence and into the area near the other fires I realized there were two or three dozen vehicles, maybe more, either burning or already burned out with only their smoldering hulks remaining. The group began, in response to cheers from the crowd, rocking the car from side to side. When they succeeded in rolling the car over onto its top, a vociferous roar erupted from the crowd. The crowd roared again when someone threw a lighted match into gasoline spilling from the vehicle's gas tank and flames shot into the air. The level of noise rose again, but this time there was a difference—it was not the cheers and roar of approval, but the shrieking and shouting sound of panic. The crowd was scattering in all directions, vacating an area where white smoke spewed from a small cylindrical object lying on the ground. The crowd pulled back from the area of burning vehicles, but shouting continued for a while, abating slowly to nothing more than a murmur; the fires were also dying down. Only one fire was shooting up flames of any magnitude. I was about ready to go home when a girl climbed onto the top of a camper shell mounted on the back of a pickup truck and began chanting

"Winnebago! Winnebago! Winnebago!" The crowd quickly picked up the chant and pretty soon everyone was shouting in unison, "Winnebago!" "Winnebago!" "Winnebago!"

I will never know if it was a coincidence that a motor home driving along the road paralleling the trees had pulled off and stopped within perhaps twenty yards of my tree, presumably to observe the bizarre activity, or if the girl had watched the motor home approach and then decided to climb onto the camper and incite the crowd. In any case, someone began pointing and shouting and within a matter of seconds a group of perhaps fifty or sixty descended upon the motor home. The driver, sensing danger, started the engine and tried to drive away, but it was too late. By this time the group had already surrounded the vehicle. The mob swarmed all over the motor home. Unable to get inside they started rocking it from side to side. Someone in the crowd yelled, "The bog wants you!" Almost immediately this became the new chant.

"The bog wants you!" "The bog wants you!" "The bog wants you!" It was about this time I noticed several uniformed men approaching. One of the men hurled something towards the motor home; another man lobbed a second object which landed in the midst of the people swarming about the motor home. As the group began to scatter, running in all directions while shrieking and shouting obscenities, I realized the items tossed were the smoking metal cylinders. I couldn't imagine why everyone was running unless they expected the canisters to explode. As the mob dispersed, the driver, taking advantage of the confusion, drove away. It was about then my eyes began to sting. The stinging increased in intensity until tears were streaking down my face. It was impossible to keep my eyes open and even when I managed, through sheer willpower, to force them open, I was unable to see. There was still shrieking and the yelling of obscenities from the routed mob, but I could tell, even though I was as blind as the proverbial bat, they were rejoining the main crowd, in the vicinity of the burning vehicles.

Whenever danger threatened I had always found trees one of the safest places and normally I would have stayed put,

101

but lately trees seemed to have turned against me and not knowing what might happen next I decided it was in my best interest to try and get home. I inched my way back along the tree limb to where it joined the trunk, then carefully and slowly climbed down. Unable to tell how far down the tree I had climbed or how far it was to the ground, I climbed all the way down, not dropping the last two or three feet as I usually did. My plan had been to follow my own scent back to the trailer, but whatever had blinded me had also destroyed my sense of smell. Still, I was determined to get home and I knew if I kept the crowd noise to my right and stayed at the edge of the woods I would eventually find the Airstream. All I had to do was get close enough to the trailer for my parents to hear me crying and they would come to my rescue.

It hadn't been easy, especially the early going when I bumped into rocks, fell into gullies, scraped against bushes, and encountered various other hazards. Even so, I pushed on unrelenting. After about half an hour the stinging finally stopped and I was able to open my eyes. My vision was blurred at first and I squinted a lot, but slowly it returned to normal.

My parents didn't pay much attention to me the next day; they seemed preoccupied and were gone most of the morning and half the afternoon leaving me locked inside the Airstream. With nothing to do and nowhere to go I lay sprawled on the back of the couch and between naps watched as the largest crowd gathered I had ever seen. People were everywhere, they climbed and sat on the scaffolding, they climbed onto the tops of the little houses, stood on the tops of cars, sat in chairs atop motor homes, and along the fence next to the racetrack they stood three deep. Others continued to wander back and forth on the road in front of our trailer.

The funny-looking little cars had been quiet most of the morning, but around noon they came out onto the track, a few at a time, and started zipping around the racecourse. This lasted for about an hour before they all left the track and, for perhaps half an hour, everything, except the loudspeakers, was quiet. Then the relative calm was shattered with the revving sounds of well-tuned high-performance engines. Seconds later, to the shouts and cheers of the crowd, the drivers urged their cars forward and began racing around

102

the track just as fast as they could go; they sounded like a swarm of angry, giant-sized, mosquitoes. An hour and a half later it was all over; the cars were silent, the crowd was leaving the park, the vendors were packing up their wares, and by late afternoon almost everyone had left. Even the race cars had been loaded onto big tractor-trailer trucks and were on their way out of the park.

We stayed one more night as did a few other campers. I went outside and climbed the tree behind our trailer one last time. I remained there most of the night watching the stars, listening to the night, and reflecting on all I had experienced in the past week. I would remember it all.

104

Chapter VIII
Racing With A Spaceship

By the end of November we found ourselves once again on Florida's east coast. This time we were southbound. My heart beat a little faster knowing we were heading in the direction of Key West and my pulse rate increased in direct proportion to the miles of pavement that passed beneath our wheels. The frequency with which I recalled my romantic encounter with Ernest increased as well, and I fantasized about another moonlight rendezvous. But, alas, it was not to be. We never reached Key West.

Halfway down Florida's Atlantic Seaboard we squeezed into a parking place at Jetty Park just south of Cape Canaveral. Jetty Park was reminiscent of the RV park in Las Vegas. Like Vegas, Jetty Park was so crowded there was barely enough room to open our trailer door.

From my observation post on the back of the couch, I could see the ocean and the strip of sand at the water's edge where hundreds of bodies were all greased up and laid out in the blazing midday sun to bake. With memories of the huge crowd at Watkins Glen still fresh in my mind, coupled with my beach experience at Grand Isle State Park when the sleeper wave almost got me, I was anything but excited about my parents' choice of campgrounds. However, my enthusiasm or lack thereof toward venturing outside and taking my chances with the multitude was of little or no consequence, since my parents kept me locked inside the trailer. My mother oiled up and joined the other sun-baked bodies on the sand while my father read, listened to the news and swapped stories with other campers. As for me, my internment limited me to eating, sleeping, and people watching.

As the winter solstice neared the path of the sun across the sky, the days, even in Florida, grew shorter. Sunbathers were driven from the beach earlier each afternoon as the sun sank below the horizon a few minutes earlier than it had on the previous day. The days were warm, but it cooled down rapidly after sunset and by late afternoon most people had exchanged their beachwear for warmer clothing and by early evening some even slipped on sweats or light jackets.

The crowd gathering at Jetty Park was considerably different from the assemblage at Watkins Glen. There were similarities, with people mingling and wandering about, and parties, large and small, with many lingering into the wee hours of the morning, but unlike at the Grand Prix, especially the Bog, the goings on here were orderly and without discord. Still, even with everyone pleasant and cordial to one another, it didn't make sense my parents would choose to camp at Jetty Park; they didn't like crowds any more than I did. So, why were we here?

This was our third night at Jetty Park and parties had started early and were now in full swing under RV awnings throughout the encampment. I could tell something out of the ordinary was about to happen. On previous nights most had already "partied out" by this late hour, but tonight, as though a spell had been cast, the crowd had found a new source of energy. Excitement, building slowly at first, then becoming a tidal wave, had swept everyone up in its ground swell until emotions were at a fever pitch; something was, indeed, about to happen, although I hadn't a single clue as to what.

106

The mystery thickened when a couple of guys from one of the nearby parties carried about a dozen chairs down to the beach and lined them up on the sand. Only a few minutes passed before another group relocated their entire party to the same area along the water's edge. I could see several others on their way to the beach, a veritable parade of folding chairs, tripods with cameras, binoculars, radios, and even television sets. The pace quickened and within an hour almost everyone had relocated to the beach. Latecomers were having difficulty finding room for a chair, a tripod or even a place to stand.

I still didn't have the slightest inkling of what was going to happen, but I had the distinct impression it was going to happen within the next few seconds. No doubt, this was going to eclipse anything I had every witnessed and I had no intention of missing it. I was wide awake and sitting on "dead ready."

A hush fell over the crowd assembled on the beach. An eerie stillness cloaked the entire encampment. The only sounds I could hear were the sounds of my parent's breathing, the hiss of the propane burner in the refrigerator and the palpitations of my own heart. When the alarm went off I jumped so high I almost hit my head on the ceiling.

My father sat up in bed, reached for the clock and jabbed a finger at it until the alarm stopped ringing. He was up to his good-natured grumbling as he watched TV and drank coffee. Although I had no idea what he was talking about, I caught phrases like "middle of the night" and "indecent hour"—referring to the time, 3 a.m.—and he questioned his own sanity, mumbling "I must be crazy." My mother, accustomed to his whimsical nonsense, wiped the sleep from her eyes and countered with "I agree."

"It was your idea." After getting out of bed my father had turned on the TV and when someone on the screen announced, "The countdown has been restarted," my parents quickly finished dressing, pulled on warm jackets, refilled their coffee cups, shut off the TV, and hurried outside, leaving me locked inside the trailer. From my perch on the back of the couch I watched them grab a couple of chairs and head off toward the beach and disappear into the crowd.

Time passed slowly. I watched and waited with infinite

107

anticipation, but nothing happened. It wasn't that I was losing interest, quite the contrary. Something colossal was about to happen and I had no intention of missing it, but as time dragged on my eyelids grew heavy and I was having difficulty fighting off sleep. As determined as I was not to go to sleep, my eyes were closed when I heard cheering and shouting coming from the direction of the beach. When I opened my eyes the sun was already up and climbing rapidly into the sky. How could that be? It was still dark outside, so how could the sun be coming up? The sun climbed into the sky at an ever increasing rate; faster and faster it climbed. I was scared. I sprang to my feet, but stood transfixed, wondering what to do. Suddenly, thunder like I had never heard before rolled across everyone and everything. The Airstream vibrated so violently I thought all the china and glassware in the cabinets would break. I could feel the couch trembling beneath my feet. Then it came to me in a flash—I knew what was happening. It was the end of the world! I ran to the only safe place I knew, my hidey-hole.

The Airstream stopped vibrating as the thunder faded away. A few minutes passed and when nothing more happened I decided to take a quick look around. I crawled out of my hidey-hole to find the sun had disappeared and it was still dark. I climbed to the back of the couch to find everything the same as it had been before the sun came up. But the sun hadn't come up, so what happened? I looked toward the beach where the crowd had gathered. They were all heading back toward their RVs. Obviously, the happening everyone had been waiting for had taken place and I had missed it. Then again, maybe not. I was confused. Perhaps a few Purina Stars would help me sort things out.

I nibbled at my crunchies, unaware of their taste, or whether or not they were fresh, or even how many I ate. I was hungry, but there were too many things running around inside my head to give food any serious consideration. Back inside my hidey-hole I tried to recall everything I had seen. I wondered what I had missed during the short time my eyes were closed. Were my eyes only closed momentarily or had I been sleeping for some unknown period? Could I have dreamt the whole thing?

108

My mother entered the trailer and started a fresh pot of coffee, then immediately turned her attention to getting the Airstream ready for traveling. I could hear my father outside, going through his pretravel routine. Why were we getting on the road, in my father's words, "in the middle of the night?" Was it because of the strange sun and thunder? Were we in some sort of danger? My father opened the door and inquired, "You about ready?"

"Just about," my mother answered as she filled two cups with hot, steaming brown liquid. After stirring heavy cream into the coffee that was to be my father's, she stowed the coffeemaker, then looked inside my hidey-hole.

"Just wanted to make sure you were okay," she said, then disappeared. I heard the door lock and the step slam up into its traveling position, and a few seconds later the El Camino roared to life and we were off.

It was several days later when I finally unraveled part of the mystery; it would be years before I fully understood what had taken place. I can tell you now, of course, but at the time I had no idea we were racing with a spaceship. I am not indicating we actually raced the three-thousand-plus miles from Florida to California but my father drove almost continually, except for the time we spent eating and sleeping in freeway rest stops.

It was not until we set up camp at Edwards Air Force Base that I began to understand what had taken place at Jetty Park. Some TV guy kept talking about how NASA had launched the first reusable space vehicle, the SST-1, at Cape Canaveral. When the TV showed the SST-1 taking off, I realized I had mistaken the powerful rocket, burning through the darkness as it climbed into the night sky, for the rising sun, and the sound of the exhaust reverberating in the early morning stillness, for thunder.

We arrived in the early afternoon and joined the hundreds of others already there. We set up on a hillside overlooking a dry lake bed and several large buildings. Beyond the buildings an airport runway extended across the dry lake bed as far as the eye could see.

By nightfall, new arrivals were having a difficult time finding a place to park. It reminded me of Watkins Glen—no organization. Lately, we had been following the crowds. I hoped it wasn't going to continue. I hadn't been faring well in crowds. It seemed anytime we stayed in a crowded campground I either got into trouble or was kept locked in the

We were ahead of the crowd when we set up the Airstream overlooking the NASA complex at Edward Air Force Base as we awaited the return of the space shuttle Columbia. By noon the following day it was impossible to find a parking place on the otherwise peaceful hillside. For some reason, the media zeroed in on us—we were interviewed by CNN, and by newspaper reporters from Oakland and Detroit.

trailer. With this in mind, I was surprised when at my first request the door opened and I was allowed outside.

I knew it unlikely I would find a climbable tree here in the desert and didn't bother looking; I was content to sit atop the

110

El Camino. The high desert air was fresh and invigorating and normally I would have already been out exploring, but once again we were surrounded by partying campers and I was determined to make good my vow to stay out of trouble.

As at Jetty Park, the merrymakers were considerate of nearby campers. There wasn't a lot of room to spread out, but as campers arrived they were careful not to intrude and to choose a spot that afforded others as much privacy as possible. This was not an area regularly used for camping and was authorized, by the Air Force, only on special occasions. We were fortunate to be given a spot on the hillside where only a few hundred campers were permitted to set up their rigs. Most were required to park miles away on the dry lake bed where at least a thousand campfires dotted the desert floor. Vehicles arrived continually, their headlights painting colorful light trails in the night. Traffic waiting to turn off the highway onto one of the dirt roads that wandered aimlessly through the desert was backed up all the way to the horizon. At this rate the number of people gathering on the lake bed would far surpass the combined totals of Watkins Glen and Jetty Park.

The sun was already high in a cloudless California sky when I was awakened by loudspeakers. "What now!" I grumbled, remembering the speakers at the Grand Prix. Grumbling was a habit picked up from my father, I suppose. Curious, I crawled out of my hidey-hole and climbed onto the back of the couch. I couldn't make much sense out of the conversations coming over the loudspeakers, but there seemed to be a lot of dialogue between a guy named Houston and someone called Columbia. I viewed the loudspeakers as a nuisance; the crowd, however, seemed very excited and listened intently to the information broadcast over the public address system. I was getting the same feeling I had had at Jetty Park, that something unusual and exciting was going to happen, and once again I was without a clue as to what.

By noon reporters from two different newspapers and a television crew from CNN had interviewed my parents; they seemed very interested in the fact that we had been at Jetty Park. With the help of the television, the loudspeakers and the reporters' questions I figured out what all the excitement was about. The SST had been shot into space, whatever that

111

was, from Cape Canaveral and was going to return, from wherever it had been, to this very spot here in California's high desert. With this realization, many questions ran through my mind.

Would there be thunder again? What about the sun? I pondered these questions and others as I watched the different types of vehicles, all with flashing lights of one kind or another, positioning themselves along the sides of the long runway. I was determined not to doze off this time. This was a second chance and I wasn't going to miss one single solitary thing. Everybody was outside, but this time rather than setting up chairs they were all standing up. Some stood together in twos and threes, others were standing alone, many clumped together in small groups. All were scanning the skies.

As time passed, conversations between Mr. Houston and Mr. Columbia increased considerably. The only lull had come after one of the two men mentioned something about a "re-entry burn." I guess there had been some sort of accident. A short time later Mr. Columbia announced the burn was complete and had been successful. Evidently, he had managed to put out the fire. His report seemed to excite the crowd. A few more minutes passed; then someone pointed to the sky and yelled, "There it is!" Everyone stared in the direction indicated and within a couple of seconds more people were pointing, yelling, and cheering. I kept looking but all I could see was a funny-looking airplane. The airplane descended rapidly as it passed overhead and continued down the dry lake bed before banking sharply in order to line up with the runway. The pilot guided the plane to a perfect landing. A loud cheer went up as the strange-looking airplane touched down and Mr. Houston said, "Welcome home, Columbia." Was this what all the excitement was about, an odd-looking airplane? Or was it a glider? I hadn't heard its engines. Where was the thunder? What happened to the sun? This was all very confusing to me. I didn't know what to expect, but hadn't expected a funny-looking airplane. Was this really a spaceship? Everyone cheered again, long and loud, as the airplane came to a stop and the first strains of "America the Beautiful" were heard emanating from the public address system. The crowd grew solemn and, as they listened, I detected many a moist

112

and reddened eye. I did not fully understand why the crowd had been so overcome with emotion, but I, too, was touched by the lyrics as I thought about the wonderful life I lived in this beautiful land referred to in the song. My parents and I were free to travel anywhere we pleased and due to this freedom and good fortune I had been able to see much of America and knew firsthand that it was indeed, America the beautiful. I wondered what would have been my lot had I been born in another place or at another time?

114

Chapter IX
Leaving Civilization Behind

There could be no mistaking the sound; it was eerie and mysterious, but it was a sound that quickened my pulse and elevated my spirits. I scanned the bright star-studded sky for a few seconds before spotting them winging along the outside edge of the moon's penumbra, two waves of big Canadian honkers. It was a beautiful sight, a sight for which I had been watching and waiting. I didn't know how they knew when it was time to set out on their annual pilgrimage to their northern nesting grounds, but I did know we, more or less, followed the geese, heading south as winter approached and north in the spring. With the Canada goose now on the wing, I knew spring was approaching and my father would soon be pointing the El Camino northward. In the north we would no longer be plagued by the crowds, peace and quiet would return. And I would be free, once again, to pit my wit and skill against nature.

We had wintered in California's beach parks. Early on we

115

camped on the Silver Stand near my birthplace in Coronado and then along the ocean north of San Diego. Now, each move to a new campground took us a little further up the coast. Twice we had left the coast: once to the desert—something to do with desert wildflowers—and the second time to a nice campsite on Northern California's Klamath River where my father fished a winter run of steelhead. Steelhead are rainbow trout that go to sea, and like salmon, return to freshwater to spawn. Unlike salmon, however, steelhead do not die after spawning, but return to the ocean. And yes, in case you're wondering, they taste heavenly.

Of all the places we stayed that winter I enjoyed the Klamath River most of all. It was the first place we had been, in what seemed like an eternity, where we were not surrounded by people. Having finished my first night of exploring, I was sitting on top of the El Camino listening to the river when I spotted a skittish little guy, about half my size, with big eyes, short fur, and dark rings around his tail. He gave no indication of having seen me, so I sat very still, hoping to find out what he was up to. He was sure an inquisitive little guy. He searched through all our belongings and even climbed onto the top of the Airstream, a feat beyond my capabilities. I had met creatures resembling the little fellow in my dreams and I wondered if somehow my dreams were linked to reality. Was I clairvoyant? Could I see into the future? My dreams or anything relative to them always left me with unanswered questions.

The steelhead run peaked a few days after we arrived, then fell off rapidly until it was hard even for my father to hook into an "upstreamer." You'd have to be pretty hungry to eat a spawned-out "downstreamer." So we packed up and headed back toward the Pacific Ocean, then turned north along the coast through Oregon and around Washington's Olympic Peninsula, stopping a day or two at a time at places of historical interest. But now, just as I had predicted, when I heard the wild honking overhead a couple of weeks ago, my parents were readying the Airstream for serious (long-distance) traveling.

We were camping on American Lake near Tacoma and my parents were laying in supplies in amounts such as I had never seen before. Both the El Camino and the Airstream were bulging at the seams with everything from dried beans to toilet

116

paper, canned soup to motor oil. And thank goodness, lots of cat food and kitty litter. I sat on the picnic table and pondered the purpose of the ugly wire mesh covering the El Camino's grill. I also wondered about the carpet hanging underneath the rear bumper. Well, I wasn't going to concern myself about them; sooner or later their purpose would become obvious. I might not have known the purpose of the wire mesh or the

On our way north from the Lower 48, Gold Pan Provincial Park on the Thompson River in British Columbia was usually our first stop. I was always excited when we camped at Gold Pan because it was then I knew for sure we were on our way to Alaska.

carpet, but one thing I knew for sure, tomorrow was a travel day. The Airstream stood hooked to the El Camino, all city utilities (electricity, sewer, and water) had been disconnected. We were now completely self-contained, and my parents were in bed early, indicating a predawn departure.

My mother was up at three; she rarely skipped her morning run. My father was up by the time she returned and within an

117

hour we were heading down a northbound freeway ramp toward Seattle. We crossed the Canadian border into British Columbia well before noon and the sun was still several degrees above the horizon when we pulled into Goldpan, a provincial park on the Thompson River. I had no way of knowing at the time that Goldpan would become one of our regular stops as we followed the annual migration of the Canada goose.

We camped at more places than I can remember on our way to and from Alaska; however, Lac La Hache, British Columbia, although a beautiful and well-maintained campground, was not a place I could get excited about. Outside I stayed close to the fire, but I spent most of my time in the Airstream sleeping, dreaming, and fantasizing about the new and exciting adventures I knew awaited me farther to the north.

We traveled slowly, some days covering less than a hundred miles and our stay at any one place varied from a single day at some to as much as a week at others. We stayed at places with strange-sounding names such as Lac la Hache, Crooked Creek, Whiskers Point, Muncho, Kluane, Tok, and Teslin. This first time around the very sound of these names was wonderfully strange and thrilling and this was just the beginning. Later there would be places with names like Nahanni, Inuvik, Denali, Kenai, Kasilof, and Ninilchik, which sounded foreign and even more intriguing. In time they would become as familiar to me as my own name.

118

We had barely passed through Dawson Creek when the pavement ended. When the pavement ended I thought we had turned off the main road and assumed we were nearing our destination, the place where we would spend the summer. I was wrong. We had not turned off the main road. It would be more than twelve hundred miles before we were to see pavement again and most of the summer would be spent driving

We traveled the Dempster Highway in the Yukon Territory two weeks after it was opened to the public. In those days a permit from the Territorial Government was required for all nonofficial vehicles traveling the Dempster. Once you turned off the Klondike Highway just south of Dawson City, the only public services on the Dempster were 230 miles away at Eagle Plains, just 20 miles below the arctic circle. We purchased fuel from road crews along the way—that was the norm. Our destination had been Inuvik; however, the ferry at Eightmile crossing on the Peel, just south of Fort McPherson, was not operating, so our journey ended in the Northwest Territories about 90 miles past the arctic circle.

on dirt roads. Dawson Creek, British Columbia, is mile zero of the Alaska-Canadian highway which ends 1,523 miles away in Fairbanks, Alaska and is known to locals and those who drive it, as the Alcan. However, anyone driving the Alaskan Highway today will find it completely paved, and it saddens me to think many will never know or appreciate the Alcan before it was straightened, leveled, widened, paved, and made virtually into just another freeway. For today's travelers there will be many emotions and adventures never experienced. Today's travelers must be content to live the events in their imagination while listening to old-timers telling stories around the campfire or by reading some sourdough's accounting of the good old days, when the Alcan was nothing more than a wilderness access to the Last Frontier.

All lakes north of Hundred Mile House—a stage stop on the "Caribou Road" nearly a thousand miles before we reached the Alaska Highway—were still frozen. Snow still lingered in

In my day the Alcan was a dirt and gravel road that snaked its way through a vast wilderness; in Alaska it was paved. I am one of the few still referring to the Alaska Highway by its military acronym which is short for Alaska-Canada military highway. The Alcan was built by the army over a period of seven months in 1942 in response to the Japanese attack and occupation of Attu and Kiska in the Aleutian Islands.

wooded areas and on north-facing slopes, but now, due to the lengthening periods of sunshine, the ground, frozen all winter, was beginning to thaw. The Alcan was beginning to thaw as well and at times was quite treacherous. Just the thaw itself made for slow going. Any additional moisture in the form of rain or snow made the road, to quote my father, "as slippery as STP." At times our rig became so heavily caked with mud I was unable to see through any of the windows. The carpet, hanging beneath the rear bumper of the El Camino,

120

became so heavy with mud and water the fasteners could no longer support its weight and it fell off, becoming just one more lost item to be plowed under by the next road grader. At other times, after a day of sunshine, dust from passing vehicles made it impossible to see ten feet beyond the windshield—headlights were required, by law, at all times, day or night. When dust flew, so did the rocks. The wire mesh did a good job of protecting the front of the El Camino and the radiator from flying rocks, but without the carpet hanging underneath the rear bumper, rocks thrown up by the El Camino's tires pelted the Airstream continuously.

Since crossing the Canadian border we had been traveling almost due north, but at Fort Nelson, a couple of hundred miles from the Yukon Territory, we turned west. As Fort Nelson disappeared in our rearview mirror and the road narrowed down to the point where I wondered what was going to happen when we met another vehicle, I suddenly got the feeling we were leaving civilization behind and only wilderness lay ahead. I cannot begin to describe what I felt at that moment. My feelings were too mixed and varied, but I do recall that excitement, above everything, dominated my emotions and I was not surprised when I noticed that the fur on my back was standing on end. When my father turned off the Alcan onto a narrow road leading into the woods I surmised that this time for sure we had arrived at our destination. But a quarter of a mile later, when the road ended at a 100-foot-wide circle, carved out of the snow by road graders, I realized we would not be staying very long. After a half dozen more stops, when each time I had theorized this to be the place where we would spend the summer, I set speculation aside and took the stops one at a time.

From the back of the couch I watched my father as he leveled our rig and heard the Airstream groan a couple of times as he cranked down the stabilizing jacks. Except for an eighteen-wheeler parked opposite us on the far side of the circle, a truck camper, and an old school bus converted into a motor home, we were all alone. By the time my father came inside my mother had coffee and hot soup ready. The soup smelled delicious and piqued my own appetite. After crunching a few Purina Stars I returned to the back of the couch, where I surveyed the snow-covered landscape.

121

Although I was half asleep and paying little attention to my parents, I was aware of their movements, so when, immediately after eating, my father pulled off all his clothes and slipped on swim trunks, my first thought was perhaps he had been smoking some of the strange-smelling tobacco I had encountered at the bog, although I knew he would never be that stupid. Before I could collect my thoughts, my mother emerged from the bedroom wearing nothing but a bikini. A couple of minutes later they were heading out across the snow and, as I watched them disappear into the woods, I came to the conclusion they had gone mad. Many times I had questioned my parents' sanity, but this time I had no doubt whatsoever. They were, indeed, crazy.

I was awakened by the sound of the key being slipped into the lock and knew my parents were returning from wherever they had gone. I wondered if their skin had turned blue from the cold; I'd heard it happens. I watched with a certain amount of curiosity as they entered the trailer. They weren't blue at all. If anything, they were sunburned and steam was rising, ever so slightly, from their skin. If I hadn't known better, I would have thought they had just stepped out of a Jacuzzi.

Whatever madness possessed my parents still lingered; they were preparing for bed even though the sun was still well above the horizon. I figured I'd better get out of the house; one never knows what crazy people might do. I stood by the door and went into my I-want-to-go-outside routine. When the door opened I bounded straight into a snowbank. Actually, it was more like a wall of ice than a snowbank. My father had positioned our rig so as to make it easy to pull back onto the little road that led to the Alcan, and in doing so, had parked the Airstream with just enough room to permit the door to open without banging it into the snow scraped up by the road graders. I bounced off the ice wall, landing on my feet, of course, and thought maybe I had bumped my head a little too hard, since the air felt quite warm. I had expected the temperature to be below freezing, but I guessed it to be in the upper sixties, perhaps even the low seventies. I set out across the parking lot to the spot where my parents had entered the woods and followed a path through the snow to a small footbridge. The water underneath the little bridge smelled strange; as a

122

matter of fact, although I hadn't noticed until now, the entire area smelled strange. I climbed down and lapped the water. It tasted the way it smelled, but to my surprise, the water was actually warm. I pondered this for a moment or two. I had never seen a warm stream running through the woods before and was curious as to its source. Thinking I would probably figure it out later I put my questions aside and ventured deeper into the woods. The path became a series of little bridges, which reminded me of the log trail in Okefenokee and I took a good slow look around for alligators before deciding it might be wise to climb one of the nearby trees until I had a better understanding of the area.

I awoke expecting it to be dark, but, to my surprise, even though the sun had dropped below the horizon there was still plenty of daylight. It was kind of like a heavily overcast day; however, there wasn't a cloud anywhere in the sky. Although daylight still remained, the temperature had dropped considerably and other changes had occurred as well, reminding me once again of Okefenokee as fog rose in little wisps throughout the woods, and somewhere further on along the trail giant white plumes towered high above the trees.

The little bridges became more numerous until in the end the trail became one long continuous bridge spanning shallow pools of bubbling, steaming, foul-smelling water. This last bridge opened out onto a large wooden deck with a covered area at one end. The planks, worn smooth over time by countless bare feet, partially surrounded a fairly large pool of the same smelly water that trickled beneath the bridges along the trail. Steam rose from the pool and a thick vapor cloud hung above it. I walked across the deck and stared down into the pool for several minutes. Beads of water began to collect on my whiskers as a current of warm moist air billowed up into my face. The water was very clear, making it easy to see the sandy bottom, about three feet below the surface. I was just about ready to leave when movement underneath the deck caught my attention. Peering through a crack between the planks, I saw several large, fat-bellied frogs, some clumped together, some sitting alone. All but one sat motionless.

Considering as how I hadn't seen any other little critters fit for eating, I decided on a frog's leg dinner and began looking

123

for a way to get underneath the deck. I walked toward the sheltered area at the lower end of the pool, where a small dam kept the water from escaping. Except for the bubbling sound at the opposite end of the pool where water seemed to boil up out of the earth, spilling over a series of discolored rocks before trickling into the quiet water below, and a loon laughing somewhere in the distance, not a sound was to be heard.

I jumped at least four feet into the air when a nearby voice called, "Kitty, kitty, kitty, kitty." I spotted the couple, sitting there in the shadows, even before I hit the deck. I landed within an arm's length of them. The couple was sitting on the bottom of the pool with their backs against the little dam with only their heads sticking out of the water. No wonder I hadn't seen them before. Well, this cleared up the question of my parents' sanity. Then again, maybe not. Normally, I would have hit the deck with only one thought in mind: Run for your life. But for some reason I didn't feel threatened.

"Kitty, kitty, kitty." the lady called again, then asked, "Wonder where she came from?"

"Probably from the Airstream that came in this afternoon, eh," the guy answered. What did he mean, came in this afternoon? Several hours had passed since we arrived, so if we'd arrived in the afternoon, why wasn't it dark?

"What's your name?" the lady asked. They seemed nice enough, so when the lady held out her hand, I took a couple of cautious steps toward her, allowing her to scratch the top of my head.

"You'd better be careful, little girl. There are lots of wolves and coyotes around. They'd love having you for dinner." Hah, she'd never seen me climb a tree; I didn't worry about wolves and coyotes. As if reading my mind the guy said, "She could probably climb a tree and get away from wolves or coyotes, but a tree won't help her if she runs into that wolverine whose tracks we saw this afternoon; it would be curtains for sure, eh."

"He's right," the lady said as she scratched my head again, "You'd better go on home." I knew about wolves and coyotes, but what the heck was a wolverine? Perhaps she was right, maybe I should go home. I said my good-byes and headed back down the trail.

By the time I reached the middle of the long bridge, the

124

light was finally beginning to fade and a weird sort of twilight cast a sinister-like spell over the woods. I thought about the couple's warning. The lady had seemed sincere when she cautioned me about the wolves and coyotes, and I remembered the seriousness in the man's voice when he mentioned the wolverine. His ominous remark, "curtains for sure" still rang in my ears. I wondered what a wolverine looked like. He was probably pretty big, big and mean.

The failing light and dense fog limited visibility. It was difficult to see from one bridge to the next. I took a quick look around and, although seeing nothing, quickened my step. I had gone only a couple of hundred yards when the loon, eerie and haunting, laughed again. The cry of a loon is one of the two sounds that paint a picture, in my mind, of everything I imagine the wilderness to be. The howl of a wolf is the only

The Liard Hot Springs in British Columbia became one of our favorite stops along the Alcan. After several days, sometimes weeks on the road, depending upon the side trips we took, my parents enjoyed soaking in the hot water that bubbled up from deep within the earth. Except for the surrounding wilderness and the contrasting night sounds, it reminded me of the hot springs in Yellowstone. My first experience at the Liard Hot Springs was quite traumatic, but I later found an abundance of tasty little critters living in and around the warm water that drained into the surrounding marsh.

other sound to come close. I kept telling myself there was nothing to worry about, but it did little to calm my nerves and I realized the hair on my back was standing on end. An involuntary shiver caused me to stumble as I leapt onto one of the bridges. When I recovered my footing, I found myself looking at the biggest, ugliest creature I had ever seen. A wolverine!

He was at least eight feet tall with a head the size of a

Volkswagen. He must have weighed a ton. It was difficult to see clearly with the fog rising up all around him, but he was there and he was looking straight at me. He stood motionless in the hot water chewing on something, part of which still dangled from his large mouth. I knew he intended to eat me next.

Instinctively, I looked for the closest tree, but remembering the guy's warning "curtains for sure" I knew a tree wouldn't help me—I was doomed! I stood frozen, unable to move. My life was over and there was nothing I could do. If a tree wouldn't save me, there was no hope. Having accepted my fate, I felt fears subside and with this subsiding of my fears came a return of rational thinking. The wolverine might eat me, but he was going to have to catch me first. When the beast lowered its ugly head to charge, my desire to live overcame my fear and I sprang to the other end of the bridge, landing in a dead run and while yelling my head off, streaked toward the Airstream. When the door finally opened I headed straight for my hidey-hole. But still, even in my hidey-hole, there was no doubt in my mind, that if the wolverine had really wanted me, nothing could have saved me.

The sound of sizzling bacon and the aroma of fresh-brewed coffee beckoned me from a deep sleep. Sleep hadn't come easily, for most of the night I hadn't slept at all and jumped at every sound, but when fatigue finally overcame my anxiety I'd fallen into a deep sleep and slept soundly. I stretched and climbed out from behind the couch to greet my parents. I knew it was a miracle I had lived to see them again or to even see another day. It felt good to be alive. My father was cooking breakfast, which meant my mother was still out on her morning run, but would be home shortly. This also meant we would be getting underway right after breakfast. Suddenly I remembered the wolverine and panicked. My mother was out there with the wolverine. A single leap carried me all the way to the back of the couch. I had no sooner landed on the couch when I spotted him standing in the trees where the access road intersected the parking lot. Almost at the same time I spotted my mother turning off the Alcan onto the access road. She was only fifty yards from the parking lot and would reach the intersection in less than twenty seconds. She was doomed! I had to warn her! What could I do? My father

126

could help her if only I could make him understand. Looking in the direction of the wolverine, I arched my back and started hissing and spitting as loud as I could. My father leaned down and looked out the window, then asked, "What's wrong with you? Don't you like the moose?" I stopped in mid-hiss and looked at my father, dumbfounded. By the time I looked back at my mother, she was passing the spot where the "moose" had stood only a couple of heartbeats ago and to my surprise, the giant creature hadn't attacked. As a matter of fact, it was lumbering away through the woods. I was embarrassed by the whole thing and felt foolish having let my imagination get the best of me, but hey, this was all new to me. I'd never seen a moose—how was I to know? Besides, wasn't it better to be safe than sorry?

My mother entered the trailer and asked excitedly, "Did you see the moose?" Well, I'd met my first moose. I didn't know anything about moose, except they were sure big, but I had a feeling it was a lot better to meet a moose than to meet a wolverine.

128

Chapter X
Little Thieves

From the Liard Hot Springs we continued almost due west along the Alcan for the next three hundred miles, passing through Watson Lake, Teslin, Johnson's Crossing, Jake's Corner, and Whitehorse. Whitehorse, capital of the Yukon Territory, has a population between ten and fifteen thousand, half of all the Territory's population, whereas other towns might consist of nothing more than a store, a gas station, and a post office—often all in the same building.

A hundred and fifty miles or so west of Whitehorse stood the old gold rush town of Champagne. Actually, there had never been any gold in Champagne, nor was there ever a real town, it had merely been a stop on the Dalton Trail—a toll road from Haines, Alaska to the goldfields of the Klondike, established and operated by Jack Dalton. The town came by its name when a couple of entrepreneurs heading for Dawson City with several cases of champagne were caught in a blizzard for several days and during the storm consumed all

129

their wares. Champagne didn't interest me, but nearby was what appeared to be a town of little bitty houses. While my parents ate lunch I wandered through the little houses. They were just like real houses, but too small to serve any practical purpose. There were dozens, perhaps hundreds, of little houses all lined up on what appeared to be little streets. After returning to the trailer I learned, through my parents' conversation, that the local Indians believed after death the spirit rests for a year before rising from the grave. When the spirit rises it needs a place to live, so during the first year either the family or friends of the deceased build a "spirit house" and place it over the grave, providing the spirit with a place to live. I had mistaken the cemetery for a town and the rows of graves for streets. All this was very interesting to me and made perfectly good sense.

The town of Haines Junction had grown up around the intersection of the Haines Highway and the Alcan. At Haines Junction we turned southeast toward Haines, a port on Alaska's famous Inside Passage. A few miles down the Haines Highway my father turned onto a very narrow, winding gravel road. Twenty minutes later we parked at the road's end beside a frozen lake.

While my father cranked down the stabilizers—my mother called them trailer feet—I looked out the windows, checking in all directions. There wasn't another vehicle anywhere in sight; we were all alone. We were parked at the lower end of a long, but fairly slender body of water or I should say ice, as it was on that bright sunny afternoon in late April. Kathleen Lake snuggled up against mountains to the south. Spruce and birch grew thick along its northern shore and the other end lay hidden somewhere deep in the Kluane range. You realize, of course, I learned the names of towns, lakes, mountains, rivers, glaciers, and so forth over many years of living on the road. Fulltiming provided for an education and understanding of life I would never have known had I lived out my days in our little yard in Bonita.

One thing that really bugged me my first summer "above the Sixty" was the lack of darkness. Even now, after spending numerous summers in Alaska, I've never gotten used to the long days and short nights. However, as that first summer

130

drew to a close—winter can come anytime after Discovery Day—things started turning in my favor and by Labor Day the length of days and nights had reversed. By mid-October we were headed "outside" (back to the Lower 48). This reversal had given me six weeks when there were longer periods of darkness and I had been able to explore during the nighttime I loved so dearly. Knowing my preference for darkness over daylight, I'm sure you understand why, with sunshine flooding the Airstream, I wasn't upset when my parents left me locked inside the trailer. For me, wandering around in broad daylight wasn't anything to get excited about. I was content to view my new surroundings from a comfortable position on the back of the couch.

Between naps I marveled at the vastness outside my window and tried to separate my dreams from reality. Sometimes they seemed one and the same. Except for the occasional caw of a nearby raven the entire region appeared devoid of life. As much as I enjoyed the absence of vehicles, noisy kids who often throw rocks at me, and the blaring radios some humans can't seem to live without, I felt a momentary touch of loneliness and found comfort in my dreams and in the relationship with the creatures, now familiar to me, always waiting for me in my subconscious world.

I had been awake for a very long time and began to wonder when my parents would return or if they would return. I knew they would never abandon me, but sometimes when they had been away for a long time I remembered what happened to Butch and I would be overcome with melancholy. This was one of those times. A great aloneness hung like an invisible fog, chilling the spirit, and at that moment I would have welcomed another vehicle, a rock-throwing kid, or even a boom box. I closed my eyes and escaped, once again, into my dreams.

By the time my parents returned there was a hint of darkness, so I ventured outside, but sat for hours on the lower limb of a medium-sized birch tree wrestling with my emotions. Lying in front of me in every direction was the unknown. Except for my parents there was not a single human to be seen or heard. This was the type of place for which I long whenever I hear a boom box, we spend a night in a

131

crowded trailer park or we're caught in a traffic jam. So why was I still sitting in a tree only twenty feet from the Airstream? It wasn't the vastness of the wilderness lying before me that overwhelmed my adventuresome spirit—it was the ominous warning by the nice couple at the hot springs and the thought of a likely meeting with the dreaded wolverine that kept me up a tree. I still had no idea what a wolverine looked like, but he grew more fearsome every time I considered a possible encounter with the beast.

Curiosity finally overcame my inhibitions and I set out along the graveled road we had driven over on our way to the lake for about a hundred yards before turning up the hill and into the woods. The day had been fairly warm, but cooled down rapidly once the sun, moving not across the sky but in a path almost parallel to the horizon, finally dipped below the mountaintops. Water, locked frozen in the earth during the long winter, thawing now by exposure to the sun during the extended daylight hours, had refrozen and crunched underneath my feet. Ice ringed the numerous puddles and frozen crystals reached out from the edges toward their centers. All this would reverse tomorrow when the sun's rays would penetrate still deeper into the frozen earth unlocking an even greater amount of water, but for now in the gloaming that passed for summer nights above the Sixty, it served as a reminder that winter is never far away. I continued up the hill until I reached a spot overlooking the frozen lake and leapt onto the trunk of a fallen tree.

Visibility was good, but deceptive, as it always is when dawn is threatening and time seems stuck somewhere between night and day. I sat watching the dimly lit stars visible in a cloudless sky, waiting for them to disappear, but hours passed and dawn did not come and the stars remained. As I watched I became aware of bands of light appearing, faint at first then growing brighter as they moved across the sky. They appeared in different shades of red and yellow, sometimes green or white. At times the light bands appeared sporadically and moved slowly, at other times they appeared frequently and shot across the sky or fell toward the earth in curtains that almost reached the horizon. During brilliant bursts of color, I associated sounds with the lights, sounds as eerie

132

as the lights themselves. The sounds were, no doubt, the wind, or a night bird on the wing or, most likely, a figment of my imagination.

I don't know how long I sat, hypnotized, marveling at the strange phenomenon when an unmistakable sound awakened me from my trance. The sound was not far away and it definitely had not been created by my imagination. It came again from somewhere just across the lake. This time the call was answered by the rest of the pack. Maybe it was because of the safety of the nearby trees, unlike the desert where there were none, or perhaps it was because I was older and wiser now—I was not as panicked by the sound of the howling wolf pack as I had been by the similar call of the lone coyote in Death Valley. Still, the wolves had my full attention. My eyes strained to see through what passed for darkness on a late April night in the Yukon. They were like shadows moving swiftly and silently across the ice near the base of the mountains. The leader had rallied his troops to the hunt. They were now on the trail of their prey and would not speak again until after the kill. I envied the wolves their ability to survive in this vast and unforgiving land. My ancestors, those in my dreams, also lived in a harsh land and hunted in groups. I wondered how wolves had managed to maintain their freedom and family order while I had become a solitary hunter, dependent upon others outside my own species. Don't misunderstand me, I loved my parents and the life I lived, but there were times—and I was unable to explain these feelings— when I desired to know if I could survive on my own, as my ancestors had done in ancient times.

The stars along with the lights began to fade away long before the semidarkness ended. It was well after sunup when I heard the water pump cycle. In the Lower 48 it always cycled around dawn. Still, the cycling water pump served as an alarm clock of sorts. It alerted me to the fact that my mother was up and making coffee, which meant I could call to her from the step and she would open the door and let me inside. After a long, leisurely stretch I headed back toward the trailer and the security of my little home on wheels.

I was no longer sure of the time. The long days and short nights rendered my standard references to time useless or at

133

best inaccurate, but judging from the position of the sun, I had slept late. I assumed my traditional position on the back of the couch and gazed out across the lake toward the mountains where I had last seen the wolves. There were no wolves to be seen, but what I did see caused my eyeballs to pop almost out of my head in disbelief. I closed my eyes for a moment to make sure it wasn't an illusion. Much to my dismay, it was not an illusion; my parents had just walked out onto the frozen lake. Why would they do such a stupid thing? Didn't they remember the time I fell through the ice? I was panicked; they were going to die and all I could do was watch.

What would I do? How would I survive without my parents? Even before the thought had clearly formed in my mind I felt ashamed; how could I be so selfish to think of myself at a time when my parents were about to die? I turned my head, too embarrassed to look at them, afraid the ugliness of my thoughts had somehow been conveyed to them and the last thing they would remember would be my selfishness and not the depth of my love. Still ashamed, I forced myself to look in their direction and watched, with a heavy heart, as they picked their way across the ice.

I remembered the first time I saw them. I was sitting in a cardboard box with my brother and sister in front of the Navy Exchange in Coronado when my mother reached down, picked me up and exclaimed, "Aren't you cute?" I was all excited—I was going to be adopted! Then my father responded by asking, "How do you suppose she got so ugly in such a short time?" It would be much later before I would understand my father's appreciation for irony, but at that moment I was crushed. I expected my mother to put me back into the box and walk away, but instead, she retorted, "She's not ugly, she's beautiful," and pressed me against her breast. I was so happy; I purred as loud as I could. I remembered our house in Bonita and my friend Butch. I thought about all the times my father had come to my rescue and about all the games we played. I realized I was crying.

When they stopped walking I blinked a couple of times to clear my eyes of tears. After pointing to something on the ice, my mother turned back and began retracing her steps toward the shoreline. They were coming back! If only they could

134

make it. My fears were just beginning to subside when I noticed my father was continuing farther out onto the frozen lake. I couldn't understand why he would be so careless; he always approached things so logically. I guess I was still crying when my mother opened the door, because she rushed over, picked me up and asked, "What's wrong?" She held me on her lap, scratched my chin and talked to me for several minutes before putting me down. I climbed up onto the back of the couch again and continued to watch my father grow smaller and smaller until he disappeared around a tree-covered point jutting out into the lake. My mother sat on the couch and watched through binoculars. She appeared pensive and ill at ease.

I was unable to nap, as I normally did during the day. Each time I dropped off to sleep scenes of my father falling through the ice flashed across my subconsciousness and my eyes popped open and I stared out across the frozen lake. I'm not sure how long this scenario continued, but now my eyes were surely deceiving me. I watched a faded old red truck moving slowly across the ice; it appeared to be heading straight toward the Airstream. As it neared the shoreline I was able to determine there were three occupants inside the truck. When the driver coaxed the vehicle onto terra firma and the door opened my heart soared. The first person out of the truck was my father.

Everything became clear when my father reached into the truck bed and lifted up a big lake trout for us to see. He eased the big fish back into the truck bed and headed for the Airstream. The other two gentlemen followed my father to our trailer where my mother served everyone hot coffee and bowls full of steaming chili with fresh-baked sourdough bread.

And so began the first of many friendships to evolve over the years with residents above the sixtieth latitude. The two men had spent more than thirty years in the Yukon and had many stories to tell about life above the Sixty. Any question my parents asked provided the men with the opportunity to spin another yarn. If one of the men's wives hadn't become concerned why it was three hours past the time her husband had promised to be home for dinner and had not come looking for him we would probably still be there listening to sourdough tales.

135

The next day we arrived in Haines and after buying a few groceries and filling up the El Camino with gasoline we followed the road along Chilkoot Inlet past the Alaska Marine Highway ferry terminal and a big sawmill before turning onto the roughest road we had ever traveled. I suspect it may have been the roughest road in the world. The road was so rough the eight wheels on our rig, without any relation to one an-

It is difficult to comprehend the vastness of Alaska, a land that constitutes 16 percent of the United States and all her territories combined. If you superimpose a map of Alaska onto a map of the same scale of the Lower 48, the Aleutians will jut out into the Pacific Ocean while the southeastern Panhandle extends into the Atlantic Ocean. So it is easy to understand how we came to Alaska, that first summer, with a long list of things we wanted to do and places we wanted to see and it is equally easy to see, many summers later, how we have yet to do half the things on that list.

other, were either going into, at the bottom of, or coming out of a hole. About a mile and a half later the road ended in a small parking lot beside a lake. After twenty minutes on the world's bumpiest road—it was impossible to go more than five miles an hour—I was about to lose my lunch, so when the door opened I was outside and up the nearest tree in record time.

I spread myself out on a nice fat limb, closed my eyes, and filled my lungs with fresh air. While waiting for the nausea to

136

pass I fell asleep and visions of Ancients, possibly my ancestors of eons past, crept across my subconsciousness. These Ancients struggled to survive in a harsh land and slept in trees to evade their enemies. When I opened my eyes it was difficult to separate the dream from reality; the panorama lying before me was so much like the dream that I checked the tree to see if I was alone. Mountains reaching up to the sky, with glacier horns at the top, ran along each side of a narrow valley. A huge glacier hung at the head of the valley where the mountains converged—a reminder of the past and perhaps, of things to come.

Below the slopes a lake reflected a mirror image of the mountains and sky above. The river flowing out of the mountains carried giant ice cakes, dumping them into the upper end of lake. The ice cakes floated down the lake and were eventually swept into the swift current of the river that emptied into Chilkoot Inlet a couple of miles away. As the ice cakes hit the rapids just below the lake they broke up with a whispered whooshing and twinkling of a thousand crystal wind chimes compressed into a single moment and a single sound. The valley seemed so peaceful, but I knew life-and-death struggles were commonplace. Still, something told me I belonged here. Were the Ancients calling to me? Was this a place where I could survive on my own? Was this my heritage?

The dreams and fancies were swept from my subconscious as something disturbed the water's surface near the edge of lake. I don't know how I chose the tree I had climbed—it might have been instinct or logic or it could have been merely by accident. The parking lot serving the picnic area was small and would have held no more than half a dozen rigs like ours. The parking lot jutted out into the water at a point just above the spot where the lake narrowed down and emptied into the river. However the choice may have been made, my tree stood just up the hill at the end of the parking lot overlooking the lake, with many of its limbs reaching out over the water. I watched a spot where a slight disturbance occurred on the lake's surface until the ripples had almost died away. Just about the time I was beginning to lose interest, the water directly below my tree erupted as a river otter popped out of the lake and climbed onto a half-submerged log. A split second later

137

two more scrambled onto the log. The first and largest of the three, had a nice shiny trout gripped firmly in its mouth. The otters were probably planning to have the trout for dinner; however, this was not to be. They had no more than settled onto the log when a giant bird with at least a six-foot wingspan swooped down on the unsuspecting otters. The huge bird was dark brown, except for its snow-white head and tail. I thought I must be dreaming again—no bird could be this big. Something, a shadow perhaps, warned the otters and at the last moment they dove into the water, leaving their dinner behind. The giant bird scooped up the trout in his talons in midflight and winged his way back across the lake to a tall tree, where he shared the trout with his mate. I wondered how many of these guys were around. Well, it would no doubt behoove me to keep an eye to the sky.

I climbed down from my tree and wandered about the woods for a while before heading back toward the trailer. By the time I reached the Airstream my father already had two of the same trout the otter had caught—he called them Dollies (Dolly Varden)—over hot coals on a grill by a picnic table. My father had caught four Dollies all together; the other two were swimming around in the lake at the end of a shroud line, the opposite end being attached to a big rock. My father was planning on fresh trout for breakfast without having to get up early to catch them, and had come up with a foolproof plan, or so he thought. The next morning when he went out to retrieve the Dolly Varden from the lake, all he found was two fish heads on the end of his shroud line. I, of course, knew what had happened. I had watched the otter family eat the two Dolly Varden.

My father, still intent on having fresh trout for breakfast, continued to cast a green and gold streamer into the lake, letting the current carry the streamer toward the river before retrieving it. With each cast he would mumble something like "good-for-nothing little varmints," and "rotten little thieves." My mother, playing her part in the grumbling game, quoted a line from Robert Burns' "Ode to a Mouse," "The best laid schemes o' mice an' men, gang aft agley, an, lea'e us nought but grief an' pain, for promised joy." He opened his mouth to comment, probably about the grief and pain he had in mind for the otters, when he hooked up with an eighteen-inch

138

trout and at that moment he forgot about everything except the Dolly Varden ripping line off the spool of his fly reel.

The Dollies were delicious. Our appetites satiated, we all sat inside the trailer while my parents drank coffee, perused publications on Alaska, read the Milepost—a must for traveling the Alcan—looked over maps and made plans for the next few days. I was content to look out the window and watch ice cakes float down the lake and into the river. It was very relaxing and I was just about to close my eyes when movement at the water's edge caught my attention. The otter family was swimming along the shoreline. They stopped and climbed out of the water just outside our trailer door. They had returned to see if my father had strung any more trout onto the shroud line. Since he hadn't planned on feeding the otters in the first place, he wasn't about to catch them another trout dinner, but he'd forgotten to untie the line from the rock and to remove the fish heads. I guess the otters figured if they couldn't have a complete meal they'd settle for a snack.

My parents had opened the windows slightly to allow fresh air to circulate through the Airstream, so when the otters began chomping on the fish heads the noise could easily be heard inside the trailer. My mother was first, besides me of course, to hear the crunching sound. She turned her head, looked out the window and upon spotting the otters whispered, "We've got company." then, in the same breath, she asked, "Aren't you guys cute?"

My father watched them for a few moments before speaking as though addressing the otters. He pretended to yell although his voice was barely audible.

"Do you little varmints know what they use to make fur-lined mittens? Thieving little otters, that's what!" He then got out his camera and took their picture.

Tired of waiting for darkness, I ventured out into what I considered the middle of the day. My explorations had taken me through the picnic area past a locked gate into the campground. Deep snow still remained under the big trees and even without the locked gate the campground would have been inaccessible for RVs and most other vehicles. After snacking on a plump vole and harassing a couple of squirrels, I felt the need for a short rest and was looking around for a choice tree when I heard a nearby disturbance. Actually, it sounded like an altercation between two of the local inhabitants. The noise soon died away as the couple took their differences deeper into the woods. Curiosity demanded I investigate. Cautiously I approached the area where I suspected the commotion had taken place. Someone of considerable size had been thrashing around in the snow, but the participants in the squabble had apparently left the scene. Knowing a bird's eye view of the area would give me a better idea of what had happened, I climbed the nearest tree, which proved to be a big mistake.

I was out on a good-sized limb and was just about to get comfortable when I looked back towards the trunk and spotted them staring at me. Two bundles of golden brown fur clung to limbs on either side of the tree just about a foot above me. At first I thought they were stuffed toys, but when one turned his head and uttered a sound similar to a bawling calf I knew they were for real. It was difficult to tell, with all the fur, but they appeared to be about four or five times my size. Although they hadn't made any hostile moves I was getting a bad feeling about the situation and instinct told me I was in big trouble. I considered my options. I could either climb further out on the limb and hope they wouldn't follow, in which case I would be trapped, or I could make a dash for the tree trunk, hopefully before they could react, scoot down to the ground and run back to the Airstream where I would be safe. I chose to run and quick as lightning, in one giant leap, I reached the trunk and started down. A couple of seconds later I figured I'd climbed far enough down and I could safely let go and drop the rest of the way to the ground, but just to be sure I took a quick look below. My heart stopped and my blood froze as I looked directly into the gaping jaws of a fur ball identical to the ones in the tree, but about a thousand times larger. Time seemed to stand still while thoughts flashed through my mind at the speed of light. This, no doubt, was the mother of the two youngsters in the tree above me. The ruckus I had heard earlier was probably the result of the mother chasing away an intruder and now she had returned to find what she considered another threat to her children.

She had returned silently on big padded feet and was patiently awaiting my descent, but now, sensing I was aware of

140

One of the great things about RV-ing is that no matter where you stop you have everything you need for a comfortable stay. And one of the great things about RV-ing Alaska is that almost anyplace you can get your RV off the road will serve for overnight camping.

141

her presence, she reared up on her hind legs and took a swipe at me with a paw the size of a snow shovel. Bark exploded from the tree trunk, just inches below me. To say I was scared and feared for my life would be the understatement of the century. I was out of options—there was only one thing do. I flew up the tree right past the two little fur balls, all the way to the top. It seemed like an eternity, but in reality it was only a few minutes before the two little guys climbed clumsily down and wandered off with their mother toward the river. I didn't move for a very long time.

Of all the sights I have seen and the places I have visited, Chilkoot Wayside will always remain my favorite. Perhaps it is because we were the first campground hosts in Southeast Alaska and I spent the entire summer there. Or it could be my countless adventures, when sometimes instinct and sometimes logic saved my life. Or it might be because of all the friendships that resulted from our hosting the campground. I suspect it is a combination of all those things, but no matter the reason, my second summer in Alaska was the most memorable.

It was later I learned that except for cubs, Alaska brown bears—coastal grizzlies—cannot climb trees. Even so, I have no doubt whatsoever I cashed in one of my nine lives at Chilkoot Wayside and I wondered, as I always did after a brush with death, just how many of the original nine I had left.

By the way, I never did meet the wolverine.

142

Chapter XI
The Last Ferry Ride

We had arrived midmorning and already a hundred or so vehicles sat bumper to bumper in long straight lines waiting to board the big blue and white Alaska State Ferry. As vehicles arrived, dock workers placed colored placards in their windshields and directed drivers into the proper lanes where they parked and waited; it would be a long wait, since the ferry wouldn't be departing until early evening.

On its way north, the ferry made several stops along the Inside Passage: Prince Rupert, Ketchikan, Sitka, and Juneau, to name a few. I had seen them all before, but the thought of seeing them again stirred my emotions. Even the sound of their names was exciting. Vehicles bound for the upper reaches of Lynn Canal were always loaded first, and since our destination was Haines, we would be among the first to board. Skagway was the only port-o-call farther north; by ferry it was a mere fourteen miles between Haines and Skagway, but for anyone choosing to drive between the two towns it was a road trip of 300 miles.

143

I couldn't have been happier when I realized the big ship tied up to pier 52 was the Matanuska—known to locals as the Mat. With the exception of the Chilkat, I had ridden all the ferries plying the waters of Southeast Alaska, and the Mat, in my opinion, was the smoothest-riding ship in the fleet, even smoother than the Columbia, flagship of the Alaska Marine Highway. It really didn't matter what ship I would be riding—I would get seasick anyway—but seeing the Mat gave me a momentary psychological lift.

I was a bit disappointed when my parents traded in our Airstream for a new 5th wheel and the El Camino for a dually. The Royals had many advantages over the Airstream; it was much roomier and more comfortable, but it just didn't feel like an RV. Another disappointment came when I realized we no longer camped in some of the out-of-the-way places I really enjoyed because the Royals was too large. One of the neatest things about the Airstream was that it would follow you anywhere you had nerve enough to take it. My father had a lot of nerve.

This was my eighth trip to Alaska. We had missed only three summers since our first Alaskan adventure. For most of those years we drove the Alcan on our way north and returned to the Lower 48 via the Cassiar, but for the last three years we had left a trailer with friends in Haines and ridden the ferry back and forth. The Airstream had long since been replaced by a forty-foot Royals International fifth wheel and

144

the El Camino had been turned in for a one-ton dually. We lived and traveled around the Lower 48 in the Royals, but smaller, lighter-weight trailers were more suitable for Alaska. We had two trailers, but since we had only one tow vehicle I would spend the trip to Haines stuck in our truck with my food and water on one floorboard and my pottybox on the other. Twice a day, when passengers were allowed on the car deck, my mother would come down and stay with me. Even so, it was going to be a long three days.

I recalled my first ferry ride as I often did when waiting to board. It had been another one of those times when I vowed to run away. My first trip on the Alaska Marine Highway had been aboard the Taku and it took only four hours of cruising to cover the ninety miles from Haines to Juneau, but that was enough for me. From Seattle the Mat would travel nine hundred miles before she reached Haines. Aside from getting sick due to the constant pitching and rolling, I had a headache caused by the screaming and whining of various pumps and motors. Added to this was the deep pulsing vibration from the ship's screws which kept the Taku in a constant shudder. This shudder was transmitted to and throughout everything on board right down to my very bones. Needless to say it was a miserable four hours. After what seemed like an eternity we finally reached Juneau, but I had made up my mind long before then to never get on another ferry. When the trailer door opened at Auke Bay State Campground, I was outside and up a tree quick as a flash. I can't remember how many times I ran away, but as always, within a few hours I returned home.

For Seattle, it was an unusually clear April evening when the Mat slipped her moorings and eased out into Puget Sound. I had no way of knowing this would be my last ferry ride. Night had fallen long before we reached the Straits of Georgia and I was already feeling queasy. By the time we cleared Cape Scott and entered Queen Charlotte Strait at the northern end of Vancouver Island where the Matanuska met the full force of the Pacific Ocean I was too sick to move or even lift my head. Almost twenty-four hours after departing Seattle the Mat tied up at Prince Rupert, Canada and during our stay in port I began to recover somewhat. Once we cleared Dixon

Entrance and were protected from the open ocean behind Prince of Wales Island my stomach began to settle and I was pretty sure I was going to live. By the time we reached Wrangell Narrows the Mat was sailing smooth as glass on the quiet waters of the Inside Passage. I ate a few Purina Stars and began feeling better almost immediately. There would be some rough water north of Juneau, but the worst was over. By noon the next day when we disembarked at Haines I was pretty much my usual self, although it would take a day or two before I regained my land legs. Until then I would weave and wobble when I walked.

In Southeast Alaska spring can last from three days to three weeks, but regardless of the length of spring, by late April there is a certain excitement in the air since everyone knows summer is just around the corner. By early May willows and alders begin showing new buds and chocolate lilies are poking their heads through patches of remaining snow. However, even in May there is an occasional reminder that, in Alaska, winter rules the land and summer is merely a respite. We were among those reminded, this first week in May, when snow began falling about an hour after we arrived at one of my favorite places, Chilkoot Wayside. The campground had not yet opened, so my father had backed our rig into the picnic parking lot next to the lake just past the boat ramp. From the top of a bedside table I watched the snowflakes float gently past the window—I dearly missed the viewing advantages of the comfortable couch beneath the Airstream's big wraparound windows. The snowflakes became thicker and heavier and fell faster and faster until everything outside the window was a white blur. Not only did the snow fall quietly, it muffled all sound until even the nearby river was silent; the stillness was eerie. My mind began to play tricks on me and I found myself contemplating the possibility that all the world outside our little trailer had been silenced for evermore.

I stared out the window and wondered what it would be like to be outside in the falling snow all alone with night coming down. With the passing of years I had become more comfortable with the notion that I really could survive in the wild as my ancestors had done and my yearning to do so was growing stronger with the passing of time. This desire was

146

further stimulated by our annual northern migration, which had a compounding effect. Each trip added to my already unyielding desire. I could no longer ignore these desires and it frightened me; it also excited me. At times I had difficulty separating dreams from reality and began to believe my subconscious adventures were real, separated only by time, and somewhere there was a door that would allow me to transcend this gulf and live in both worlds. Were my dreams real? Had I already, unknowingly, found the door? Did I actually live in two worlds? Recently, my answer to these questions, more often than not, was yes.

I continued to sit as though hypnotized and stare out through the window, seeing nothing. My thoughts strayed beyond logic, where reality and fantasy collide. I imagined a doorway somewhere amid the ice crystals that fell so softly as to muffle all sound, a doorway through which I could pass into the ancient world I now visited only in my subconsciousness. Night came, or what passed for Alaskan nights this time of year, and my emotions were tugging me in all directions. I wanted desperately to go out into this quiet night, out into a totally new experience, out to search for the door, but I stayed inside our little trailer where I was safe and warm. I reasoned that I had not yet fully recovered from my three-day ferry ride and needed the extra rest, when in reality I lacked the confidence to venture out into the ghostly stillness.

The click of a solenoid, the hiss of escaping propane, and the resulting detonation as the pilot ignited the furnace all served to break the silence and bring me back to my senses. Was I going mad? Perhaps, but other things concerned me even more. My enthusiasm had not diminished, but my body did not respond as it once had. Aching joints, failing vision, and at times a shortness of breath discouraged me from many activities. I no longer flew up trees as I did in my younger days. Nor did I wander for miles in a single night of hunting and exploration. Something was happening to me and I didn't understand. I pondered these developments for several minutes before closing my eyes and entering, once again, my parallel world.

I slept late, again. In days past this would have been a rarity, but lately it had become the norm. The snow stopped

147

sometime during the night—the only evidence the freak storm ever existed was the wonderland outside my window. A bright sun shining down from a clear blue sky reflecting off the newly fallen snow forced an involuntary squint as I looked out across the pristine landscape.

My mother finished putting plates, flatware, a tablecloth and napkins into a brown paper bag before slipping on her Juneau sneakers, aka Ketchikan tennis shoes (black rubber boots). She spotted me watching her as she opened the door and asked, "Want to go outside?" I stood up, stretched and walked toward the door. When I hesitated upon reaching the door, she reached down, picked me up, and carried me across the parking lot to a picnic shelter and put me down on one of the tables. My father had a fire going in one of the grills under the picnic shelter and was busy watching over the contents of a couple of cast-iron skillets and two sixteen-inch Dollies cooking over the glowing embers.

The tables and most of the area underneath the picnic shelter were clear of snow. I took another long, leisurely stretch before sitting down on the table. My father came over and while scratching my head began harassing me. I would have been disappointed had he done otherwise.

"Well, if it isn't the Fatbee and how are you this afternoon?" His reference to my weight might have been justified, since I did eat well and often, but I knew he was putting me on about the time of day. I hadn't slept all morning. I started purring and tilted my head backward, coaxing him to scratch my chin.

"Why aren't you out pestering little critters? Snow too deep for you?" I could understand why he might ask such a question. I rarely went out in the snow. It was at Bryce Canyon where early in my travels, in the wee morning hours just before dawn, I saw my first snowflake. While out hunting and exploring I had wandered a considerable distance from the Airstream when I noticed white fluffy stuff falling out of the sky. I was quite excited at first, but the excitement didn't last long as I soon discovered snow is nothing more than delayed rain. The snowflakes stuck to my fur without any discomfort at first, but my body heat eventually melted the fluffy ice crystals and turned them into water, which soaked

148

through to my skin. By the time I got back to the trailer I was wet through and through. Since then I've learned much about keeping warm and dry when wandering about in snow. Among other things, I learned I could stay relatively dry by stopping every so often and shaking the snow from my fur. I

Traveling to and from Alaska was an adventure in many ways, and so was the weather. We were usually on the Alcan before the last of April and didn't head "outside" until late August or early September, which meant we were never surprised at the road conditions. Sometimes, when it rained, the road turned to mud, as slick as STP, to quote my father. And then, after a day or two of sun, dust would fly so thick that after we passed another vehicle, I could not see past the El Camino. When traveling the Alcan during those months it was not unusual to be reminded, by a snowstorm, that winter rules the north and that summer is a mere respite.

was at a loss to explain why I had been unable to muster the courage to venture out into last night's storm, but I was no longer intimidated by snow as I had been on that night in Bryce Canyon. I had known for some time, although I couldn't explain how I knew, snow was part of my destiny.

As if to show my father he didn't know as much about me as he thought, I jumped down from the table and bounded off through the two-foot-deep snow toward my tree—since the day I first climbed the big spruce I'd considered it my

149

tree. I had taken only a half dozen leaps when my father called out, "You're not going to sneak-up on any little critters acting like a rabbit." I continued on toward my tree as though I hadn't heard. I suppose I did resemble a rabbit hopping along, but leaping carried me through deep snow faster and it was a lot easier than walking. I reached my favorite limb before he called out again.

"What's that noise I hear?" He put his hand behind his ear, as though listening for some faint sound, then yelled, "It sounds like mice laughing." He continued with his good-humored harassment. I delighted in the attention, but pretended not to hear him. After standing for a few moments, with his hand shading his eyes as thought straining to see and while peering at the base of a nearby tree he exclaimed, "Yep, it's mice laughing alright. I see one rolling around on the floor of his little house holding his sides to keep them from splitting." I had to admit, he could be clever at times.

We spent the summer on the Kenai Peninsula. My father caught and canned salmon, caught and froze halibut, dug razor clams and was now busy collecting and drying mushrooms. My mother filled jars with jams and jellies made from the different kinds of berries growing in Alaska and was now gathering and drying wild rose hips. I had spent my time hunting, exploring, napping and dreaming. I couldn't remember when I had enjoyed myself more. Time passed quickly, too quickly. Before I realized it, summer was nearing its end—north of the Sixty winter can come, without warning, anytime after Discovery Day. (Gold was discovered in the Yukon Territory on Rabbit Creek, renamed Bonanza Creek, August 18, 1896.) Even during the years when summer lingers, "Termination dust" can be seen on the upper mountain slopes by mid-September. Termination dust—light snow—is a warning to all those heading "outside," by way of the Alcan, to make haste and for those staying behind to get all their ducks in a row (Outside is a term used by locals to mean anywhere in the United States outside of Alaska, usually referred to as the Lower 48.).

It was with this in mind that the forty or so people eating a potluck supper around the campfire in space 57 of King Salmon loop in the Russian River campground made plans. Many were Fulltimers, like us; others were only summertime

150

RVers and came to the Kenai each year to fish, can salmon, and visit with old friends. All were headed for the Lower 48 and would drive thousands of miles before reaching their destinations. One couple had towed an Airstream all the way from Miami for eighteen consecutive summers. Some would be leaving the following morning and by the end of the week only a few, waiting for a run of silvers (coho salmon) would

I spent some of my most enjoyable and carefree days camping on the Russian River. Back then the Forest Service maintained and managed the park. It was hardly ever crowded and there were no paved roads or paved campsites. Moose, bear, porcupine, and grouse, as well as low-bush moose (snowshoe hare) and other critters wandered through our campsite and there was always an abundance of mice and squirrels—I thinned their ranks from time to time. And in those days fishermen were allowed to keep rainbows and Dolly Varden as well as salmon, so we ate fresh fish every day. Needless to say, I always added a little weight whenever we summered in Alaska.

still be around. The Russian River, where the term "combat fishing" was coined, was more than a great fishing hole; it was a meeting place for old friends and a place where strangers became friends. Several made plans to visit one another during the winter, but above all, everyone planned to be back next June for the first run of Russian River reds (sockeye

151

salmon). At that moment, I had no way of knowing I would not be returning to the Lower 48, would never see the Kenai again, nor taste another sockeye.

We departed the Russian a few days after the last big cook-out and headed for Anchorage, where we prepared for the 2,500-mile trip to Seattle. My parents, having decided a small

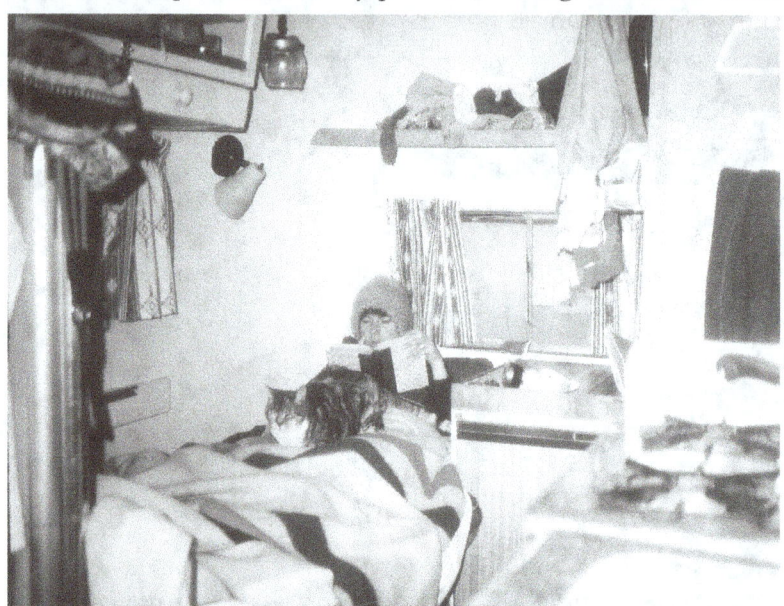

Bambi, our boondocks trailer, was very different from the Royals. It was small and cramped with hardly any place to sit. Sometimes, when it was really cold outside, our little propane furnace could barely keep up. Its one advantage was that it allowed us to get off the beaten track where few others dared to go, so it is easy to see why I had mixed emotions when we switched back and forth between the two. I loved the versatility of Bambi, but I also loved the luxury of the Royals.

motor home would be more practical for Alaska, were taking the trailer outside, where my father would fix it up for resale. Personally, I was glad to see it go; of all the trailers we'd lived in I liked this one least of all. The Royals was great; I could lie on the big king-size bed and look out the front window as well as both side windows. But my favorite was our first Airstream. Not just because of the wraparound front windows and the comfortable couch back, but because it had

152

introduced me to Fulltiming. I had looked back from time to time and remembered all the places I'd been, the things I'd seen, and the exciting times I'd had, but with summer winding down, it seemed to me past adventures crossed my mind more and more frequently and were becoming more meaningful and realistic. My dreams were taking on greater meaning as well, and sometimes I had difficulty separating dreams from reality and yesterday from today, as dreams, memories and reality often merged as one. I was vaguely unsettled by it all, but I didn't know why. What did I not understand?

A couple of days after leaving Anchorage we intersected the Alcan at Tok and set up camp beside the river a couple of miles east of town. I knew we were no longer moving, but I had trouble walking since the trailer floor still seemed to be in motion. Frost heaves on the Tok Cutoff, between Glennallen and the Alcan, kept our rig pitching and rolling like a rowboat in a hurricane. It swayed so much I was beginning to believe we were back on the ferry. By the time we reached Tok I was sick as the proverbial dog, and when the door opened I headed for a tree and some fresh air.

My parents were all set to go off in search of shaggymane, but when I refused to come down out of the tree my mother decided, rather than leave me alone, she would stay behind and let my father hunt inky caps by himself.

I knew my mother really wanted to go mushroom hunting and I would have come down from the tree, but I was too weak to move. Something strange had happened to me. I had barely reached the first limb when pain shot through my chest and down both front legs. I felt dizzy and had a hard time breathing. It became difficult to focus on my surroundings; everything became devoid of color and I'm not sure, but I may have lost consciousness. Time passed and eventually things returned to normal, or at least as normal as they had been for the past couple of months; my energy no longer matched my enthusiasm.

Hunger pains had replaced my nausea. It was Purina time. I stood up, stretched, extended and sharpened my claws, then climbed down the tree. My mother sat in the sun reading *The Great Alone* and upon realizing I was heading for the trailer, put her book aside, got up from her folding chair,

153

walked over, and opened the door for me. As I entered the trailer she closed the door behind me, strapped on a day pack and set off to find my father.

We spent two nights in Tok. On the morning of the third day we were on the road early and for the first time in over four hundred miles we were heading south. Driving from the Russian River Campground to Anchorage one travels almost due north and from Anchorage to Tok the highway runs northeast, but at Tok, if you're headed outside, you turn southeast on the Alcan towards the Alaska-Yukon border.

By the first of September, the long arctic days and short nights of summer were rapidly reversing roles; this was of

It was easy to tell when it was time to start thinking about the trip "outside." Nights grew longer, extra sweaters were worn around the campfire during the day, and my father limited his fishing so as to catch just enough trout for the evening meal. Cases of canned salmon were already put away ready for traveling. It was a sad time for me as I turned my thoughts to what lay ahead—traffic on city streets, noisy campgrounds, and the lack of room to roam and hunt.

course to my liking. As evidence of this phenomenon, it was still early in the afternoon, but the sun was already low on the horizon. My mother sipped hot coffee while she and I waited in our trailer outside a bank in Whitehorse. My father was inside the bank exchanging American dollars for Canadian dollars—we would need Canadian money for our trip

154

through the Yukon and British Columbia. It was here my mother did the strangest thing. I was lying with my head in her lap while she stroked my fur when, for no reason I could discern, she set her coffee cup down, picked me up and carried me outside. She then held me above her head and slowly turned three hundred and sixty degrees as though she wanted me to have one long last look at Whitehorse. Did she know something I didn't know? Afterward, she held me very close for a long time.

It was almost dark when, a hundred miles later, we stopped for the night at Marsh Lake Territorial Campground. During our stay at Marsh Lake I spent every minute outside, mostly sitting on the picnic table. I listened to the night sounds, breathed in the cool, fresh air, watched the northern lights play faintly across the sky and wished I could stay. But I knew I would never leave my parents; I would return with them to spend the winter someplace in the Lower 48, where I would dream and wait for the day we would head north once again.

It was two days later that my father eased our rig into a pullout beside one of my favorite places. The picnic area lying between the Alcan and Teslin Lake was one of the more isolated stops along the highway. Except for a small Indian settlement and hunting camp nearby, there were no humans within a hundred miles. This was my kind of place. I knew the area well—whether northbound or southbound, we always stopped at Teslin Lake. The door opened; I was out like a flash and with newfound energy sprinted up a nearby spruce. I was within two feet of the first limb when the pain shot through my chest. My legs stopped working. Everything began turning black and, unable to hold on to the tree trunk, I felt myself falling.

From the position of the sun it was obvious I had been unconscious for a considerable time. I still lay where I had fallen and surmised I had been sleeping. I got up and after a nice long stretch found the pain to be gone. I had never felt better. I decided to climb the tree again. I climbed without any effort at all; it was as though I had willed myself up to the limb. Nearby movement caught my eye and I turned my head to see my mother walking within a

155

few feet of the tree where I sat. She called out to me and I answered her immediately, but she kept walking as though she hadn't heard me. When she called a second time I answered in a louder voice, but she continued walking. I called to her as loud as I could—still, she did not respond. Was she going deaf? She was only a few feet away, but kept walking as though she hadn't heard me. I watched as she wandered aimlessly through the picnic area and along the shoreline; every so often she would stop and call out

Each year by summer's end my father's beard filled in enough to give him the look of a full-fledged sourdough, but once outside and back in the Royals, he shaved it off and took on the look of a city slicker.

156

my name. I sat in the tree, puzzled, and wondered why she hadn't heard me. As she neared my tree for a second time I waited until she was almost underneath, then called out to her again. She gave no indication of having heard me. As she approached the spot where I fell out of the tree I heard her call out my name, but there was something strange about the way she said, "Honeybee." It was a sound of someone in pain. Her legs gave way and she fell to her hands and knees. She was hurt—I had to help her. I was

Once "outside" and back in the Royals, my parents changed their dress and the way they looked. Perhaps it had to do with the weather, but no matter the reason, my parents dressed differently and looked different in Alaska from in the Lower 48.

about to vacate my limb when something caused me to hesitate. I heard her call my name again, in the same pained voice, "Oh, Honeybee." No, it wasn't exactly pain I heard in her voice, it was dolefulness I detected as I listened to her repeat my name over and over.

It was then I noticed she was stroking my fur. I blinked my eyes several times and looked again; sure enough I still lay where I had fallen. But how could that be? I was up here in the tree. This was very strange. I continued to watch, not moving, as my mother took me in her arms, got to her feet, and carried me into the trailer. Yes this was strange, indeed,

157

too strange to be real. Well, of course, that was it. The answer was obvious—it wasn't real, it was a dream.

I remained in the tree, waiting to wake up. But I didn't wake up. A short time later my parents exited the trailer; my mother still held me in her arms. My father removed a short-handled shovel from the truck and followed my mother over to my tree. My mother pointed to an area underneath my tree, then sat on the ground and held me on her lap while my father dug a hole on the exact spot where I had fallen. When my father finished digging he took me from my mother's arms and placed me in the hole. I noticed he took great care to situate me in my favorite sleeping position. He then re-moved my collar and slipped it into his pocket. All the while, my mother sat on the ground crying. I had to go to her. I climbed onto her lap, but she didn't move.

Things were beginning to make sense. She didn't move because she could neither see me nor hear me. It was, in-deed, a dream, but not your ordinary dream. I had found the doorway that opened into the world I had known, until now, only in my dreams. I had sought, found, and passed through the door, but there was something I hadn't counted on. It was a one-way door; I could never go back. It was at about this time I realized I could move about the tree with relative ease, doing things squirrels could never do—as you know, I al-ways envied squirrels their ability to climb and move through the trees with such ease and grace.

I climbed effortlessly back onto my limb—it required nothing more than my desire to be there—and watched as my father shoveled dirt over my earthly remains. When finished he placed a large rock on top of the mound of freshly disturbed earth, then turned to my mother and helped her to her feet. They walked slowly toward the truck. My father opened the passenger's door and helped her onto the seat, waited a few moments, then closed the door. After stowing the shovel and locking the trailer he opened the driver's door and climbed in behind the wheel. I watched their every move and I knew it would be a long time before they would be a part of my life again.

I couldn't believe my parents were really and truly leaving me behind. I watched as my father, looking straight ahead, eyes moist and reddened, trying to be strong for my mother's sake, started our big two-tone brown truck and pulled back onto the Alcan. Our little blue and white trailer, one of the five in which I had spent the last twelve years of my life and traveled half a million miles, followed along behind, bouncing through the chuck holes in the pullout beside Teslin Lake. I could see my mother crying, looking back until they were out of sight.

Even though I had never considered that someday they

Whatever the occasion called for, whether a wedding, a picnic, or a summer in Alaska, my father looked the part and dressed accordingly.

might leave me behind, I have no regrets. They were the best parents anyone could have asked or hoped for and they provided me with an extraordinary life and above everything, they always loved me. I will never forget my parents; their memory will remain with me forever. Oh, I'll be melancholy

159

for a while, but the pain will pass. I have a beautiful new home amidst birch and spruce with rock roses scattered along the lakeshore. There will be plenty of food; already I've spotted several fat voles playing in the fireweed. I'm looking forward to the many new experiences to come.

The leaves on the birches have already turned golden, the nights are getting longer with each passing day, and there's termination dust on the surrounding mountains. Soon I will be able to listen to the wolves chasing caribou across the frozen lake and I can play and hunt by the light of the aurora borealis to my heart's content. This is the free and independent life I have longed for, a life without bounds, a life I've known only in my dreams. Now, at last, my dreams and reality are one and the same.

There are many things to think about, many plans to be made and next year, when my parents return with my spirit house, it will all begin. But, for now, I'm very tired and I need a long rest.

The end.

www.ingramcontent.com/pod-product-compliance
Lightning Source LLC
Chambersburg PA
CBHW070041260626
47159CB00005B/2098